AF225635

Jingle Hell
A Rather Disturbing Christmas Carol-ish Tale

BOOK ONE
OF THE BATTLE FOR SOULS SERIES

JINGLE HELL

A Rather Disturbing Christmas Carol-ish Tale

MAGNUS HUFFAM

FRANCIS HINTON PRESS

Published by Francis Hinton Press
Designed by Faust Ltd.
Pazuzu, Lamashtu and Murmux illustrations by Mary Lempa

ISBN (paperback): 9781642377729
eISBN: 9781642376449

To Steph

�✻✻✻✻✻✻✻✻✻✻✻✻✻✻✻✻✻✻✻✻✻✻

For those who care, or perhaps even worry about such things, on March 28, 2018, a 93-year-old Italian journalist and self-professed non-believer named Eugenio Scalfari published an article in the Italian newspaper La Repubblica *that suggested Pope Francis denied the existence of Hell during a conversation between the two of them. The story was picked up extensively by mainstream media and set off a social media firestorm.*

The Vatican quickly issued a statement describing the meeting as "private." The statement also said Scalfari's article was "the fruit of his own reconstruction" in which the pope's words "are not cited textually." The statement further warned that the article "should not be considered as a faithful transcript of the Holy Father's words."

Vatican watchers promptly pointed out that Francis had indeed spoken of Hell in the past in a way that clearly indicates he believes in it. For example, in 2016 he said that people who do not embrace Christ will condemn themselves to Hell. Also in 2016, he referred to Hell as "the truth."

✻✻✻✻✻✻✻✻✻✻✻✻✻✻✻✻✻✻✻✻✻✻✻✻✻

DECISIONS

As I sat in my cell, I remembered the night I had struck the deal that landed me there. It kept playing on a continuous loop in my mind.

I had been obsessively worried about my gear getting stolen. It had happened once before. Both my guitar and amp had been ripped off and I had wandered around for weeks checking pawnshops. No trace. Poof. I had felt so violated, like two long-time friends had been taken from me. They weren't really worth that much, but they had been with me forever. Never again, I had promised myself.

The night was moonless. I was coming back from a show, walking down an alley I probably shouldn't have been in. I just needed to get to the van so I could lock my stuff up and go hang out with the band. I was maybe fifty feet away from the street at the end of the alley when a man perfectly pale and dressed in all black stepped out from behind a dumpster. He looked like Johnny Cash on meth, and his eyes appeared to be empty black sockets. A feeling of dread crept over me like a fresh gasoline spill nearing a flickering flame, and somehow

I knew that this guy wasn't interested at all in my gear. As I realized later, I was about to make the worst deal of my life, with my soul serving as cosmic collateral.

I shook my head, pulling myself back to the present. I stared at the cell wall in front of me. Of course, you only had the chance for this kind of thinking when there was a little lull in the action. No demons tormenting you, no blast-furnace pedicures, no year-long human taffy pulls on the rack. The moaning, screams, and cries for clemency never abated completely. But there were slightly more quiet periods, which I believe simply equated to demon down time.

The flying, dismembered head came down the cell block corridor screaming, "Another Day in Paradise, Hellions!" Another day of torture, and no snooze buttons allowed. I tried to find one on that flying head not long ago, but grabbing it gave you something akin to third-degree burns that lasted for days. Or what felt like days. Time is hard to track in Hell, and most of its residents would agree it's not a particularly wise thing to do anyway.

"*'Tis the season*," I thought to myself. I did know that today was Black Friday. Like so many of my current neighbors, I hadn't cared too much about holiday shopping when I was topside, as we all called the Land of the Living. Those happy, sappy, ridiculous holiday-themed ads and the keeping-up-with-the-Holly-BS-Jolly-Joneses part of it. But in the last couple of years since I had been tapped for this reality show gig, it had become my absolute favorite holiday.

And, well, truth be told, it was really the only holiday that mattered anymore, given the fact that I was about to enter my third *Jingle Hell* competition. I was a real rock star down here, but I knew that this time the stakes were much higher than ever before.

CHAPTER 2

LAVERNE

As a former rocker in life—the power chord crashing lead guitarist for the heavy metal band Glütenfreake—I still thought how things could have been different. If only I hadn't fallen for the GDHD (Give the Devil His Due) operative in that alley. He had really seen this naive, Iowa-born sucker coming. Well, his proposition had sounded like a good deal at the time. All that Catholic school for nothing.

I had pretty much been desperate for approval my entire life. Mom and Dad barely knew I existed, given their Evenings with Alcohol and the fact that life had disappointed them to the point that tuning out was their favorite extracurricular activity. I couldn't remember many good times. Warm and fuzzies? Not so much at that tiny little ranch home.

I'm sure that some of my issues could also be tracked back to my ridiculously uncool sounding name—Laverne—which I found out later in life from some exquisite groupie in Omaha was the name of a Roman goddess who was the patroness of minor criminals.

After looking into it further, I discovered that at one point my lame name became popular for both boys and girls based on a mistaken belief that it is similar to the word for "green" in romance languages. So maybe my parents thought "spring" when they heard the name Laverne. Instead, they were branding their child with a handle that evoked pickpockets and petty thieves, as well as gender confusion.

Now look at me. A true celebrity in Hell who as Dirk Hammer (my *nom de music* topside) had been on my way up the ladder, playing mid-level venues, seeing a couple of *Rolling Stone* mentions. Then an inglorious, drunken, Darwin Award worthy accident on a Segway landed me in the land of the eternally damned.

To make matters worse, my rather comical demise (being pitched over the grips of the Segway into a busy freeway does look a tad funny, to be fair) had been plastered all over the internet. One of the headlines was, "Band Frontman Bites the Dust in San Bernardino."

Perhaps unsurprisingly, there was nothing the Prince of Darkness liked better than a death that made a hell-bound human look silly.

CHAPTER 3

RECRUITMENT

My first recruitment meeting with Satan about two and a half years ago was more degrading than getting booed off the stage at a dive bar in Dubuque.

"Nice move on the Segway, duuuuuuuuude!" he cried with delight (and a slight Jersey accent) as four heinously hairy, scowling security demons led me into the cavern-like throne room the size of an NFL stadium. As he jabbed hand horns into the air as if he were at an Aerosmith concert, sulfuric puffs emitted from his armpits and video of my gin-fueled Segway fail played on something that looked like a 200-foot-wide TV screen. "Wooo hooo, Laverne! Nice WORK Lah-Lah-Lah Verne! You landed on the—and he sang the next three words—*Highway to Hell*" as AC/DC would have put it!" With that, he snorted and guffawed so hard that a security demon was blown into a granite column.

"Didn't realize you were a Longhorns fan," I said, trying to bite back my anger. I did manage to keep myself from making a wisecrack about his unusually small hands.

"How droll," said Satan as he gathered himself, giggling. "For years I have been fielding questions about the University of Texas football fans. You'd be surprised at the deals I *have* made down there, though," he said conspiratorially. "They love love LOVE their football in Texas. But given your creative reputation in the music world, I would have expected more from you Dirk. I mean, how many people can write lyrics like, '*I am your heat, I am your burn, I am your ache, I am your churn.*' I have to say, you have some fans down here in the afterworld." Satan tilted his head and almost smiled.

I softened at this unexpected flattery. "Well, that's pretty cool of you to say, Lucifer."

My body was immediately enveloped in unbearable pressure and heat.

"FIRST OF ALL, I AM NEVER *COOL*!" A look of incredible disdain came over his face. "AND YOU *WILL* USE MY PROPER TITLE WHEN ADDRESSING ME—LUCIFER, PRINCE OF DARKNESS!" he raged. "ALTERNATIVELY, YOU CAN USE 'ALL POWERFUL SATAN,' 'THE MOST EVIL ONE,' OR THE ACRONYM LPOD. LIKE GOVERNMENT BUREAUCRATS AND MILITARY ACROSS THE GLOBE, WE IN HELL ARE *PERFECTLY HAPPY* WITH ACRONYMS!" In a quieter voice, he added, "I'm not very fond of APS or TMEO, though. LPOD works fine. And 'Devil' or 'Satan' are simply too familiar to be appropriate."

The demon to my left whispered, "He's been on the acronym kick ever since he heard the President of the United States is called POTUS by his henchmen."

Now on the cavern floor, I felt cooler almost immediately and stopped writhing.

"Now get up," said LPOD, rolling his eyes as he looked over his shoulder. "I have a proposition to make."

I stood shakily and put a steadying hand on a security demon's head. Yes, they are that short. He looked mildly annoyed and bared his pointy teeth but bore my weight. I loved getting away with stuff like that. He knew what would happen to him if he disrupted the proceedings. I've heard of demons being buried neck deep in the Field of Sorrows for over a month and a half just for giggling during an LPOD rant.

"We have a program here in Hell that I personally find extraordinarily entertaining, and—I daresay—inspiring," began LPOD. "All great organizations have great cultures, and we in Hell are no different. The program, which *really* puts the BLACK in Black Friday, brings our own very special culture to life!"

I sat there and listened to a pretty forceful recruitment speech for about ten minutes or so. When he was done, he glared at me and said, "You will give me your answer by tomorrow." At that the Most Evil One levitated and swept out of the room with all of the security demons rushing after him.

"LPOD's on the move!" the demons called out over some supernatural radio frequency. As if he needed security, anyway. What an ego.

Oddly enough, I was left completely alone. I didn't have the faintest idea of what to do. This had never happened before. LPOD's offer had thrown me for a loop, but this was by far worse. What should I do? Wanderer around Hell for a while and take in the sights? Try to hide?

I was just getting comfy with such possibilities when, about 30 seconds later, I heard a rumbling shout from down the hall: "You idiots! Someone take him back to his cell!"

CHOICE

Things had started simply for me. I grew up in a fairly small, quiet Iowa town of about 45,000 people called Ankeny. Although no one I knew could figure out why, a prominent magazine once called it one of the top ten best towns in America for raising a family. Another magazine had ranked it 62nd in their list of the top 100 places to live.

Suffice it to say that they didn't ask me for my opinion when they concluded these things, and that my experience was just a tad different. The only notable thing I remember from my time there was when we made the national news. The local spice company donated nine tons of past-the-freshness-date garlic salt for use in melting ice and snow on local roadways. The entire town smelled like an Italian restaurant all winter long.

We had little to no money when I was growing up, which made things simple and actually pretty good in a way I recognized only later. Everyone else I knew was generally in the same boat. Because my parents were pretty checked out of my life and I had no brothers and sisters, things were oddly quiet. I didn't really like school, but I was never really pressured to work harder or worry about it. I remember having acne and feeling awkward, but I was always pretty contented and hopeful that I would make my escape after high school. I very seldom worried about much.

I discovered the guitar at around 11 years old and found that it came pretty easy to me. I spent a LOT of time playing guitar. I started getting guitar magazines. I wore guitar T-shirts. In my teenage years, I began to fantasize about making it big. I got a tattoo and some piercings. Standard fare.

It's funny what happens when you wake up one day and realize you are at least good enough at your craft to call yourself a musician. It makes you proud in a way that others will never understand. Rock musicians in particular hold a very special place in American culture, and they know it. Even the lousy ones.

But I guess you become a true rock musician when you get in a band and start getting paid to play. *That* makes you cocky, but at the same time extraordinarily vulnerable because you are now so dependent upon the approval of others. You are part of an exclusive club, albeit one that is generally ruthlessly competitive. But no matter how geeky, how nerdy and how uncomfortable you are in your own skin, you now have a superpower.

And that is exactly what gets you into hot water. (Or even hotter places.) It's the celebrity equivalent of those things called amuse-bouche— those itty bitty appetizers they serve you when you show up at a nice restaurant. You have a tiny bit, and then you want more. Then you do really dumb things, like ordering $200 bottles of wine.

Hell provides a lot of time for self-examination. In fact, it isn't eternal damnation, but eternal *reflection* that is the worst thing on offer. As I assumed was the case with most of my fellow residents, I realized that I had lived a life of profound miscalculations. They had started small, with a high school interest in the occult that was driven by my discovery—and subsequent obsession with—some 70s bands, as well as my choice of oddball bandmates. Other things followed, and eventually I made that deal with the GDHD operative. And of course my decision to ever jump on a Segway is on my personal Oops list.

My road to Hell was also paved with my belief that I generally could manage and manipulate my way to an induction in the Rock and Roll Hall of Fame. My inspiration was the saxophone-wielding geek David Robert Jones, who had evolved himself by sheer force of will into David Bowie.

I had really studied Bowie, who had decided to make it and then actually did. He had told his parents at age 16 that he intended to be a pop star. His mother's reaction was to arrange for him to work as an apprentice electrician. Thanks, Mom.

Because I had reflected on all those bad choices and bad deals—especially the one I made with that Johnny Creepy Cash guy I met that dark night—I knew I had to consider the offer that LPOD had made in his recruitment speech carefully. He had said it was optional, yet highly recommended. I supposed that meant that if I didn't do it, I was likely to get the H-E-double-toothpicks-in-the-eyes treatment, or something like that.

But then a switch flipped for me. It's time to start winning again, dammit, I thought to myself. For some reason, I was confident this was my big break—a relative term to be sure when your return address was 666 Demon Drive.

"I'll be awesome at this," I said out loud. "All I have to do is get people to be more evil. This should be a super easy way to score some special privileges in this damned dump. And then I'll actually get to hang out with some other people, at least for a little bit."

One of the surprising things about Hell is that you don't spend your time watching poor souls writhing in agony, gnashing their teeth and spewing ear-melting profanities. When I had asked one of the staff about that, he said, "Well, it used to be like that, but then we realized it was getting too entertaining for some of the eternally damned. Can't have that. Now shut up or I will impale you."

LPOD's offer was an intriguing one. Be a part of Hell's own reality-based show for the viewing pleasure of LPOD and his staff of millions. The truth was that the choice was easy. I couldn't quite believe my good luck. I was getting a shot in Hell to be in show business again. This was going to be big.

I grinned from ear to ear in the darkness.

PAZUZU

Pazuzu is one of 14 former angels who became LPOD's chief lieutenants when he led the rebellion against heaven. After that mother of all dustups, they were all cast down into demonhood.

The Sumerians, Babylonians, Assyrians, and other Middle Eastern cultures worshipped him as king of the demons of the wind. In addition to wind, he was also associated with storms and pestilence. Regarding the latter, he always appeared to have a particularly soft spot for locusts. The ancients most often believed him to be a winged lion, but they also portrayed him as a scaly human figure with ram's horns and a scorpion's tail, and that description is fairly spot on.

Of course, who can forget Pazuzu's somewhat more than 15 minutes of fame in the *Exorcist* films. His work—particularly in the first installment—might justifiably provoke the question of why demons are not eligible for Oscars.

Aliases

✳✳✳✳✳✳✳✳✳✳✳✳✳✳✳✳✳✳✳✳✳✳✳✳✳

Anzu
Bringer of Disease
Deliverer of Drought
Dark Master of the Four Winds
Southwest Wind Devil
Imdugud
King of the Air Demons
King of the Evil Spirits of the Air
Lord of Fevers and Plagues
Udug
Zu-Bird

Abilities

✳✳✳✳✳✳✳✳✳✳✳✳✳✳✳✳✳✳✳✳✳✳✳✳✳

Pazuzu can:
✳
Manipulate winds ranging from microbursts to hurricanes
✳
Create and control other weather elements such as storms
✳
Destroy millions of umbrellas
✳
Teleport
✳
Summon other demons
✳
Shapeshift
✳
Fly
✳
Spread disease via gaseous miasmas

✳✳✳✳✳✳✳✳✳✳✳✳✳✳✳✳✳✳✳✳✳✳✳✳✳

iNSTRUCTION

Before my first appearance on *Jingle Hell*, the show's two producers had lined up all of the contestants on a narrow path that ran through a pool of orange molten lava. Bubbles kept popping and splashing our legs, causing us to cringe, whimper, and moan.

We were all sneaking looks at one another. By the way, I challenge you to try not to stare when you are looking at other residents of Hell. It's not easy. It's amazing who you see in that place. I really didn't have much use for history class in high school, but I could have sworn that was Genghis Kahn near the end of the line to my right.

Keeping my eyes off of the producers was easy. I had learned by trial and error not to make eye contact with demons. If they caught you, they tended to single you out for additional terrors. Once, a demon wearing a red apron had suspended me two feet over a continuously stoked Weber grill for a month and just sat there staring at me and smiling the whole time.

"All right, you pitifuuuuul creatuuuuuures, listen uuuuuup," said the taller demon, Pazuzu. His voice was carried by an airy exhalation that sounded like a strong wind. "You will ahhhhll be pahhhhhhrt of a team, but you will ahhhhhhhhll ahhlso operate independently," said the demon-producer with his wings flapping. "'For those of you who haaaaave joined us more recently, *Jingle Hell* is ahhhhhh little like 'Survihhhhhhvohhhhhr' but actually you have ALREAHHHHHHDY been voted off of the island and your goahhhhhl is to get ohhhhthers to joihhhhn you!" He giggled for what seemed to be forever and then appeared to catch himself.

"Hhhhhhhey, stohhhhhp looking at each other! Faces dowhhhhhhn!" he shouted, when the Genghis Kahn dude was caught gawking down the line and waving at someone. The demon spat what looked like blood into the lava pool and cursed. "Listen uhhhhhhhp, you cursed ones!

"Our playing fielhhhhhd for this year's cohhhhhmpetition is Chicahhhhhgo in the United States. As you ahhhhhll know, it is called the Windy City ...."

"Pazuzu!" cried the other, smaller demon. "That is irrelevant to the competition! Just because you are Dark Master of the Four Winds—"

"Be quiehhhhht, Melchom!" shouted Pazuzu. "We don't have tihhhhhhhme for thhhhis!" He then quite unmistakably broke *his* wind.

"Wait, aren't you the Pazuzu from *The Exorcist*?" I asked, with what I hoped was a starry look in my eyes. "Wow, it's so cool to meet you!"

Pazuzu's wings flapped appreciatively. "Well, I wasn't aaaaactually in the film, of course, but the demon wahhhhhs loohhhhhhsely patterned on me." He tilted his head toward me and smiled a fangy smile.

Melchom rolled his eyes.

I hoped that flattery worked as well with this demon as it had with others I had encountered. "Seriously, without you, that movie would have been dull as day-old donuts," I said. "Wow, I had no idea I was going to meet you when I signed on to this gig."

Pazuzu grinned in a manner that was clearly meant to be pleasing but somehow wasn't. Then he turned back to the others and continued.

"You will each be ahssihhhhgned to one of sihhhhx teams of sihhhhhx," aspirated Pazuzu, "and you will have sihhhhhx hours in your location to do maaaahhhhhximum damage in terms of incihhhhhting eeeehhhhvil." He giggled involuntarily, and a belch slipped out as he convulsed. He gathered himself and said, "The wihhhhhning team will be determined by a diahhhhhhbolical instrument that has been in use for millennia in Hehhhhhhl. Behold! The Evilohhhhmeter!"

With that, Pazuzu pointed his claws to a dark portion of the cavern. A violent wind came out of nowhere and lifted the corner of an enormous, dusty, black curtain. The curtain flapped a bit and then dropped away, revealing an enormous, Jules Verne-ish contraption of dark metal tubes, gears and springs, as well as pieces of what looked suspiciously like old bicycle and car engine parts. It stood at least five stories tall and glowed with a red light from within. At the very top was a ten-foot tall black gauge with a large needle that looked like it was made of ancient, wicked knife blades.

What a cool stage set THAT would have been for my band. Some crazy pyrotechnics were all you'd need to .... Actually, it sort of reminded me of what Maim Squeez used on tour years ago. But that looked like the size of a friggin toaster compared to this thing.

"The Evilometer can measure minute fluctuations of depravity, vileness, and ill-intent," said Melchom in his snippy manner as he peered over his thick glasses. "As the paymaster in Hell, I can tell you that it is infallibly accurate and will provide us with an absolutely indisputable read on how your teams are impacting the unsuspecting mortals. We've been using it to calculate annual demon bonuses for quite some time now."

MELCHOM

MÈTRE DE 0,95c
SOPHISTI
MELCHOM
A la
bonne foi
KILO 900g
L. B.
JALLAULT

Melchom is a duke of Hell. He was a major deity of the Ammonites, a people formerly occupying territory that is today part of Jordan, until King David and the Israelites chased him out of the area. Despite the stature accorded to him by the rather easy-to-fool Ammonites, Melchom is a lesser demon. He serves as Hell's paymaster. He is often depicted as carrying a large wallet, or what many of us would now call a man purse.

The Jamieson, Fausset, and Brown Commentary on the Whole Bible notes, "The Ammonite god is said to do what they do, namely, occupy the Israelite land of Gad." And gadzooks no, that is not a typo. The Gad were one of the tribes of Israel who, after the Exodus from Egypt, settled on the eastern side of the Jordan River. Melchom was a usurper-king.

Rabbinical tradition depicted Melchom as a bronze statue of a bull heated with fire. In the chest of the bull were seven cabinets, or chapels. But as everyone knows, all clergy tend to embellish.

ALIASES

❋❋❋❋❋❋❋❋❋❋❋❋❋❋❋❋❋❋❋❋❋❋❋❋❋

As described in Jacques Collin de Plancy's Dictionnaire Infernal[1], Melchom was also known as Moloch and Melech, which in Hebrew signifies a king. Melchom, of course, was their unholy idol.

ABILITIES

❋❋❋❋❋❋❋❋❋❋❋❋❋❋❋❋❋❋❋❋❋❋❋❋❋

Melchom can:
❋
Do long—very long—division and multiplication without a calculator
❋
Haggle with the best of them
❋
Flawlessly forge documents
❋
Break into any soul's mind and squeeze out its innermost secrets (a good way to ensure embezzlement will never be a problem in Hell)
❋
Track the evil productivity and output of all of Hell's servants
❋
Command particular power in the month of December, according to some 16th century accounts. Merry Christmas, Happy Hanukkah, etc.

❋❋❋❋❋❋❋❋❋❋❋❋❋❋❋❋❋❋❋❋❋❋❋❋❋

[1] The Dictionnaire Infernal is a book on demonology, and it describes demons organized in hierarchies. It was written by Jacques Auguste Simon Collin de Plancy and first published in 1818.

Turning to a flame-licked map of the United States that was drawn on what looked like animal skin (at least I hoped it was animal skin), Melchom grabbed a pointer and slapped it down on the city of Chicago. "We will insert each team into a retail location in the Chicago metro area. You will have freedom to operate inside that location, but will be barred by Hellpower from leaving the premises. While you are there, you will have the soul-whispering ability that we demons have, which enables us to nudge humans into doing evil. Humans still have free will at all times, so this is a true sport. It is only those of extremely good conscience and sound soul who are generally able to resist us. And frankly, those in that category become fewer by the decade."

The other demons chuckled and nodded.

"The points will be tallied by the Evilometer, which I have tuned to be infallible, so no petty griping about the scores or you will be punished severely," said Melchom.

"But how do we get out of Hell and into Chicago?" asked a soul who appeared to have been a British army officer. Pazuzu turned on him and with a casual gesture seemed to flick a lightning bolt at him. Everyone stared in stunned silence. The guy was gone.

"I wahhhsn't expecting to cuhhhht anyone from a team thihhhhhs quihhhhhhhckly," said Pazuzu. "I'm suhhhhhhre Colonel Pearlybohhhhhttom will enjoy his new puhhhhhnishment. Noooooo-one will EHHHHHHVER learn of exactly hhhhhhhow we gehhhht you into the lahhhhhhnd of the lihhhhhhving," Pazuzu said. "Suhhhhhfice it to sayyyyy that we will handle the trahhhhhhsnportayyyytion, and when the time is up you will be returned to Hehhhhhl. Any other curious caaaaaats in the grouhhhhhp?"

Most of us stared down at the oily black cavern floor.

"The winning teahhhhm for each show win a sehhhhhlection of fabulous, super coohhhhhl prihhhhhzes curated by LPOD himself," Pazuzu continued. "Past prizes have included the 'Lawrence of Arabia treatment'—a glahhhhhhss of lemonade

with iiiiiiiiice—(Pazuzu copped an airy Peter O'Toole voice
as he said it), a cohhhld shower and evehhhhn—imagine
ihhht—a snowcohhhhhne!" At that, a tall blonde man in
line who was wearing a black Nazi SS uniform grinned and
excitedly clapped his hands like a little child, then appeared to
remember himself and looked down quickly.

"But certainly, the best outcome for any of you would
be to know that we, the demons and other minions of Hell,
recognize your accomplishments and thoroughly relish the
idea of watching you drag humans just a tad bit closer to The
Pit," said Melchom. "That alone should make you intensely
proud." He smiled.

Some of the contestants in line were clearly into that. They
grinned and nodded. A guy in a bad suit who looked like a
used car salesman grinned maniacally. I thought to myself,
this is going to be big—REALLY big. And a blast.

"Please don't expect to see the program itself, however,"
said Melchom. "We always have questions on that topic. But
that would be too much like the other 'H' place. After all, you
cannot expect us to entertain you down here."

Just then, LPOD levitated into the room with a swarm
of security demons in tow. "Don't mind me, everyone! I just
wanted to see how all of you handpicked recruits are doing!
Black Friday is soon to be upon us! Is everyone as excited
as I am? I'm expecting some GREAT entertainment from
your efforts." Then his expression turned grim and his voice
rose to a bellow. "And if you fail me, YOU WILL KNOW MY
ULTIMATE WRATH AND OBLIVION!" He brightened again.
"But I'm sure this will be the absolutely best Black Friday show
ever!" And he disappeared in a burst of brimstone and fire.

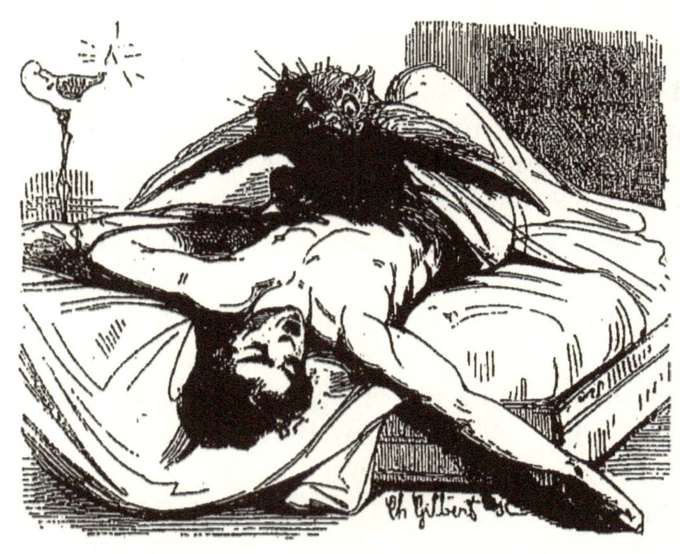

TALENT

I was ridiculously nervous. It was the same kind of jittery thing that I used to feel before gigs. The gnawing stomach, the excess energy that made me feel like bouncing off the disgustingly filthy, dripping, steamy walls of my Hell cell. Any moment now the Black Friday competition would begin.

The talent on Team Brimstone—my team—seemed solid. The demons had explained that to be truly successful you didn't want clowns like Hitler or Stalin on your team. They just weren't team players. When Vlad the Impaler played the game, Melchom said he sulked and "didn't contribute." He certainly didn't understand the subtleties of cultivating evil in the masses. Instead, what the demons looked for in a five-star *Jingle Hell* recruit was the type of person who on Earth was a master manipulator—someone who wasn't just focused on racking up their own perdition points. I realized that, as an entertainer, I was perfect for the role.

This was just like filling up an arena with fans, like getting thousands of new Facebook friends and Twitter followers for Glütenfreake. Heck, it was like convincing my parents that it was their idea to let me go to an R-rated, sex-filled movie when I was 14.

Everyone on our team seemed as excited as I did about this big bake off. We had met briefly during the training session, so I still didn't know all that much about them. But here is what I did know.

There was an outgoing, oddly sort of charming former real estate developer named Roger, a.k.a. "Sticks" (LPOD once commented on how cool it was that he was named after the river in Hell), who had spent his career putting up strip malls in Florida and cheating (a lot) on both golf and his numerous wives. There was a very pretty, curly-haired Silicon Valley tech entrepreneur named Simone who had apparently developed a rather robust penchant for violating consumer privacy. The Genghis Kahn-looking guy I mentioned earlier was apparently not Genghis Khan, but don't ask me for his real name. There was no way I could remember the series of grunts I heard when they introduced him, but there was no "Genghis" or "Kahn" uttered to the best of my knowledge. The next member was a guy with a really long French name that sounded like it included the word "bidet." He most definitely looked like a pirate, but without the hook or peg leg. Last but not least, there was an obnoxious, sullen boy named Floris. He appeared to be both Dutch and a first-class a-hole.

If I hadn't been in Hell, I might have found Simone hot. Unfortunately, though, that kind of heat didn't translate so well to Hell. You felt the urges but couldn't do anything about them. So you just spent your time trying to stay away from the *other* kinds of hot things.

At the beginning of the training session, LPOD had taken me aside and made me an unexpected offer. "You know, when it comes down to it, Dirk, that song—'The Devil Goes Down to Georgia'—has always *really* bugged me. I'm thinking that you can come up with a new version in which the truly obvious occurs and I kick Johnny's butt." His eyes glowed.

He also told me that he felt pretty strongly about removing one part of the lyrics. "How absolutely absurd, Dirk," LPOD said as he rolled his eyes. "As I am sure you know, I can't hold rosin! It would melt! And I only play carbon fiber fiddles. Maybe you could work that in?"

"Of course, LPOD," I fawned. "How ridiculous that you might not be the victor in such a musical jam! And I'm sure that on the ax you could make Steve Vai look like an arthritic orangutan," I bowed, rolling my eyes up out of sight on the downswing.

LPOD stared at me suspiciously for a couple of seconds, and then slowly said, "We'll see how you do. If you please me with your cover you will find it worth your while. Otherwise, I'll arrange for you to be worked over with some real axes!" He made a sardonic open-mouth smile. I gulped and floundered as I stuttered out more flattering remarks that I can't even remember.

CHAPTER 7

JUMP

It was probably only a couple of weeks later that I was with my teammates as LPOD started giving us a schmaltzy pep talk while floating back and forth along the line of us. I thought I was in pretty good stead with the guy because I had already knocked out that cover and performed it at a bizarre sort of kegger LPOD threw for GDHD operatives who had surpassed their soul quotas. Well, I guess you couldn't exactly give them an all-inclusive Mexican vacation.

"We prize you more than any of your other soul inmates down here ..." he paused dramatically, his eyes passing slowly across the contestants, "because you SPREAD evil! We applaud you all and are with you in spirit on your quest!" The imps and attendant demons applauded heartily like a foul-smelling glee club.

What a moment, I thought to myself. I felt like I was once again about to shoulder my go-to guitar—a black Schecter Tempest complete with cool looking sigils inked onto the body with Liquid Paper—in front of a screaming crowd of hundreds. Well, maybe a hundred if I was lucky in the old days, to be honest.

"Now, gather your strength and cunning, because before long it's off to the races for Black Friday!" Satan roared encouragingly.

We were led off to our cells. I sat there on edge for hours. Even though I knew I could be a master manipulator, I had a hard time settling down, knowing what I faced. Then, just as I thought I would go crazy, I heard a demon shouting outside of my door, "IT'S A GO! SADDLE UP AND LET'S GET TO THE JUMP POINT!"

My heart leapt as the door swung open on its massive, creaking hinges. I saw two particularly gruesome looking dudes wearing fluorescent vests that said "SECURITY." Security demons only seemed to wear these vests on very special occasions. Behind them were Simone, Sticks, Genghis, and Floris—who was looking sour, morose, and still very weird—at the rear. Simone gave me a cute, surreptitious sideways smile and a thumbs up, which totally made my decade. Sticks looked like he was about to pitch a new strip mall project. Genghis grinned from ear to ear and pumped his fist.

"NO TALKING. LET'S GO," the lead demon growled. We trudged down the filthy iron catwalk. If you have ever seen pictures of Alcatraz, just think about if the cell blocks there were miles and miles high, pitch black, and not nearly as perfectly formed. The Hell cells were built into rock, of course, and it wasn't as if anyone cared about straight lines down here. You couldn't even see the very top levels from where we were travelling.

After a hike worthy of a Marine Corps boot camp, we stopped at a door with a skull and crossbones on it. There was more demonic yelling and banging, and before too long Pirate was in tow as well.

Walking through the cell blocks of Hell is an awe-inspiring thing. Sometimes you even see souls you think you recognize, although it is hard to know for sure. As I mentioned, history was never my thing, but once in a while I thought I recognized people who had been involved with some pretty bad stuff in the past. There were a LOT of souls sporting Nazi uniforms, for example. A lot of them looked like pompous politicians. There were also a surprising number of souls in sports uniforms. Apparently hard work, talent and a spritz of performance-enhancing drugs weren't the *only* things that got you ahead in pro sports.

"Put on these hoods," said Security Demon #1. And if we see anyone peeking, you're automatically disqualified and condemned to 1,000 years of pain and suffering that will make your stay to date seem like a hangnail."

"Rooight, and I will be very happy to begin your 1,000 years today," said Security Demon #2 in an English accent.

We submitted to the hooding, then were told to grab the hand of the person next to us. I lucked out entirely and got to hold Simone's. Her hand was silky soft, yet she had a nice, firm, confident grip, despite the situation. Personally, I felt like throwing up even though I hadn't had a meal since right before my death. We then began walking, and after what seemed liked miles of twists and turns, climbing up old nasty metal ladders and crawling through very low tunnels, Security Demon #1 announced, "We're here, you louts."

Our hoods were removed and we were looking at what appeared to be the battered fuselage of a World War II-era transport plane of some sort set into a stone wall. A faded black cross was painted on the side. "Get in there and sit down on the benches," said Security Demon #2. "We're dropping you in Shopmart, so you blokes have really lucked out! If you can't foynd people susceptible to evil there, you can't foynd them anywhere! And you get to work the parking lot as well as the store! That's where a good deal of fun can be had, to be sure!" Both demons nodded and looked at each other knowingly, then snorted and laughed.

I should say that most demons do snort when they laugh. It does little to terrify people, of course, and it actually helps endear them to the residents of Hell in some small way.

Team Brimstone entered the creaking old plane and sat down on the benches bolted to the fuselage. The small space smelled of fear. The demons entered the plane through some other opening and took seats in the cockpit. They put headsets on and settled in to business. The pilot and co-pilot seats were modified for the demons' bulk. They didn't have a view through a windscreen, but were faced with a wall of instruments, dials, and levers. Security Demon #1 flipped a large, brass toggle switch on his left to the up position and the instrument panel began humming and the dials brightened to a glowing slime green. The demons appeared to be gingerly—and clumsily— pecking at keyboards with their nasty looking claws.

"Damn little keyboards," Security Demon #1 muttered.

I heard a faint tune played by what sounded like a cello. Something like *da dee, da dee da dee da dah dah dah* .... I recognized the music almost instantly. It was *Salut d'amour*, by Sir Edward Elgar. I had once spent a Saturday afternoon with my band creating a metal version of the piece.

I had long before come to the conclusion that nothing in Hell is an affectation. There was no interior decorator of Hell. Everything you saw belonged in one of two categories. Either it was just part of the natural netherworld—the lava, the rocks, the impenetrable, utter darkness of the place, or it was just sort of there without following a particular plan. And everything was old, broken, dirty, dank, and dreary not because LPOD and his demons were aficionados of some sort of underworld shabby chic.

I looked across the aisle and down the line. Everyone else was—like me—anxious and looking pretty much scared stiff. Well, except for Simone for some reason. She looked relaxed and confident. When I thought about it, though, it was a tad odd that any of us were worried at all. What could be worse than being condemned to Hell? I caught Simone's eye and she gave me a lopsided grin and mouthed soundlessly, "Awesome," with her eyes glinting and eyebrows waggling.

I glanced at my other teammates. Sticks smiled meekly and cringed a bit at some turbulence. Genghis looked sick to his stomach. This was clearly more technology than he liked. If the transport had instead involved horses, I was sure it would have been more to his taste. Pirate was grinning happily—a

natural for rough rides, I thought to myself. And Floris, was—
well—Floris was still very, very creepy.

Suddenly the plane began lurching violently. I heard a
slight gurgling noise from above. I looked up and for the first
time noticed a four- or five-foot-wide hole that became slightly
narrower as it passed up into the darkness. Then all the lights
went out except for floor illumination strips that ran down the
aisle and the glow of the cockpit instrumentation. A red bulb
blinked on to my right.

Security Demon #2 looked over his shoulder and bellowed,
"GET READY! STAND UP!" He pointed to me. "YOU'RE FIRST.
GET UNDER THE HOLE." He pointed to what I had been looking
at in ceiling. I moved there and then looked up. I could see
absolutely nothing past the first two feet or so, but I did again
hear a faint gurgling sound. It sounded like it might be water.

I glanced back over my shoulder, and as I did the red light
near the front of the cockpit went off and another one next to
the door glowed green. The plane lurched—hard this time.

"GO GO GO GO!" Security Demon #2 yelled in a voice that
made me snap my head back and look around for someplace
to actually GO. The door of the plane remained closed, so any
thought of jumping was mercilessly put to rest. Then I felt
my entire self being sucked up into the hole in the roof of the
plane. There was an incredible whooshing sound as I passed
up and in. Then everything went dead quiet and dark. For the
first time since I had heard about this whole gig, I felt raw fear.

 UP

Now why in the world I would have thought you would *jump* in order to leave Hell and get topside is beyond me. Who knows what is below Hell, but my bet is that it gets pretty molten down there. No, we definitely went *up* when we went through that hole. But I would have never guessed how they got us into Shopmart. Let's just say that pipe in the roof of the plane, after passing through what seemed like zillions of twists and turns, ended up terminating in a pretty unglamorous part of the store. A place where pipes are. A place you don't really want to visit at Shopmart unless you absolutely have to. Because it isn't so pleasant. Even for dead, incorporeal people. Who have no sense of smell. Not cool at all.

CHAPTER 9

EMERGENCE

While in the pipes, I recalled everything that I could about Shopmart. I was plotting, strategizing, getting my game face on. I remembered having checked out a "Shocking Scenes from Shopmart" YouTube channel when I was in high school. The videos showed amazing scenes of shoppers who looked like frantic, hepped-up hyenas that had descended on Shopmarts of Christmases past. With music tracks playing old standbys like "Hark the Herald Angels Sing" and—of all things—"Silent Night"—these deal-hungry crazies tore into Midnight Madness deals. Clawing, shoving, pushing. Frenzied faces, feverish eyes, frayed nerves.

I had felt sorry for the Shop-Martians, the name my friends and I had bestowed upon the stores' employees. None of us wanted part time jobs there in high school. And now, if I had to hazard a guess, their night was about to become a little rougher than they ever expected.

Just then I was disgorged into the wildly, incredibly bright Shopmart men's room. Although the colors were of course bland to those who walked the land of the living every day, the brightness of the place astounded me. I was particularly taken with the pink urinal cakes. But it was about to get much, much more interesting than that.

CHAPTER 10

SHOWTIME

After my scatologically bizarre arrival, I was a little slow to go. I passed through the restroom door and found that I was staring at what looked like paradise. The pink urinal cakes (oh to just once get a whiff of those!) were gorgeous, but the store itself was just packed with color and light. Another big attraction as compared to my current permanent address was that people were not experiencing constant pain or agony. How little they knew about how good they had it! I was not a big fan of this place when I was topside, but honestly, what was there not to like?

My completely idiotic time wasting was brought to a panicky end when I saw Floris floating into the children's clothing department. He had an odd grin on his face, and he was running his hands down the front of his shirt over and over again.

That broke me out of my reverie. I got to work. The demons had explained soul whispering as if it was one of the easiest things in the world, and despite my doubts, I found that it really was. You know those cartoons where the little devil sits on someone's shoulder and encourages them to do evil? Well, it's just like that but you don't sit on their shoulder. You just sidle up next to them, put your mouth to their ear and whisper evil thoughts into their vacuous heads. One's native language doesn't even matter, because you've got a soul-to-soul connection. I never had so much fun. It also made me wonder about something. Whenever people get the urge to be an asshole, think the worst, hate their neighbor, kick a dog, or even kill someone, might they be falling prey to a soul whisperer?

Our team had six hours, six minutes, and six seconds (hokey, I know, but dem's da rules) in total to work the Shopmart crowd. Within the first ten, I had gotten an early thirties mom to really and truly hate the heck out of a grandmotherly lady who had made the fatal error of not moving quickly enough through a housewares aisle. All it took was the following suggestion: "Why in the world is that stupid dolt blocking your way? By the time you get past this sad excuse for a speed bump, half of what you're here to buy won't even be left on the shelves and your lousy, ungrateful family will HATE you for being such an incredibly lame gifter, AAAAAAAAND it is ALL HER FAULT!"

I had no sooner finished delivering those memorable lines when early thirties mom slammed her cart into grandma and a red light and a check mark pulsed in my field of vision. It was as if I were wearing virtual reality goggles. I had just scored a point.

Perfect timing. Almost immediately, I heard a yawning girl of perhaps fourteen say to her mom "I HATE Christmas! And this place and all these people SUCK." Now why was this girl in tow at this hour? I floated over. Within two minutes, I had racked up another two points. A mother/daughter two-bagger.

Man, I *did* feel like I was winning again. Excitement, confidence, and some sort of soul-firing adrenalin were rushing through me. I had no idea how this all worked, but I didn't care. I didn't understand how we got there, how we were sharing our thoughts with the members of this mindless rabble, and how the demons in Hell were somehow tuning in to our exploits. But it was wonderful!

I kept racking up points, flitting from one person to another. I picked off a big, extremely hairy-armed guy wearing a nasty old, pitted-out Chicago Bears t-shirt in the automotive supplies section by simply noting how annoying some high-net-worth guy in designer jeans looked. Designer Jeans James made the right choice and just walked away from what could have been a pretty nasty encounter with Harry Arms. Easy peasy lemon squeezy.

I racked up a couple of points by encouraging two sisters to engage in a nasty, hateful squabble over who gave the other the best gift last year. I got one couple to fall by getting the woman to simply realize how her husband was rather clumsily checking out the other women in the store. Domestic disaster in aisle four! I mean, man, it was a cake walk.

Out of the corner of my eye I saw the other members of Team Brimstone. They seemed to really be leaving it all on the field, working fiendishly fast and efficiently. I saw Pirate stop for a moment to suspiciously eye a shelf stocked with Pirate's Plunder sugary cereal, but just for a second or two.

Pirate and Genghis were clearly focusing on the section of the sporting goods department that bristled with guns and knives. I was actually a little surprised as to how many shoppers were thinking that weapons under their tree was just the thing. Or, "Hey! Hanukkah Harry brought me a Glock!"

Floris appeared to exclusively focus on the children's clothing area. Later I learned that Sticks was working the parking lot, where he caused at least eight car accidents by inciting aggressive drivers. One melee inevitably involved more than 20 shoppers. I never went out there because the pickings were so good in the store, but I heard employees talking about it. I also heard the sirens when the police arrived. They were apparently forced to taser some of the most violent shoppers.

Perhaps most interesting—and impressive—to me was the kind of chaos Simone was causing in the electronics department. The former tech entrepreneur was certainly leveraging her deep understanding of consumer behavior to generate hand-to-hand-combat-level demand among those shoppers. It was like CNET meets WWE.

When the timer hit 6:06:06 exactly, the inexorable pull of the plumbing kicked in. I tried to fight it, like an idiot. I was having too much fun. And at that moment, I was having especially good luck in the beer and wine aisle. As my soul was drawn to the porcelain throne room, I took one last look at the Shopmart. My team's Soldier Field. Our Wrigley. No cheering crowds of course, but plenty of fun and on-field excitement. Cubs and Bears, eat your hearts out. Happy Hellidays, people. See most of you soon in *my* neighborhood. I chuckled to myself.

At that very moment, a customer service Shop Martian with a "NATE" nametag looked like he was trying break up a fight between two senior *ladies*—er, women, certainly not ladies—who had squared off over the last Oil Of Palms Holiday Moisturizer Gift Set. One of the ladies was just winding up to clock the poor guy in the side of the head when my soul got sucked down through the door of the john and then down into the ...

CHAPTER 11

RECKONING

Garf. What a nasty way to travel, even for a soul headed back to Hell. I even preferred the crappy, stinky van that my bandmates and I had used when we first got rolling with Glütenfreake. At least we could look out the windows, and it had nothing to do with raw sewage.

We found ourselves back in the old plane. Compared to the Shopmart, the darkness was stifling and utterly smothering, but—oddly enough—I felt like I was home. As we looked at each other and grinned (except for Floris), Security Demon #1 said, "Nice job, you guys." He thumbed a claw at #2 and said, "We sort of hate to give it to you, but that was a pretty incredible performance."

On the way back, the Security demons were oddly nice to our team, letting us whisper to one another. Until you spend your days in Hell in solitary confinement other than during torture time, you really don't understand how nice it is to talk with others, especially people you think you actually like. I spoke with both Sticks and Simone, who both fell into that category. I heard more about the parking lot—there was a story about someone getting hit over the head with a ham. I was blown away by Simone's successes. And of course, I couldn't help but brag a bit about my own. Pirate and Genghis seemed to somehow be communicating with each other—the *Mongol-French Connection*, I thought to myself. Floris just kept his head down and had a strange smile on his face. He wouldn't make eye contact, which was fine by me.

Although the anxious hike to the plane had felt like it took weeks, the walk back seemed to take a blissful twenty minutes or so. It was the happiest I could ever remember being in Hell. But at a certain point it began to be clear that we weren't being led back to our cells. As we wove through dark, greasy looking tunnels lit by eerie torches, jumping across molten lava streams here and there, I began to suspect we were being taken back to the Evilometer Chamber. I cringed, remembering that malicious pool of bubbling lava and how those bursting bubbles had singed my shins.

As we rounded a corner I could see the entrance coming into view. The first thing I noticed was the light. It wasn't the garish, in-your-face retail blast of a Shopmart, but it was a good bit brighter than I remembered. In fact, it was actually really, really bright (for Hell, anyway). I saw that the lava was still glowing orange, but towering over the scene was the Evilometer, and that bizarre contraption was pulsing a bright red-orange. At the very top, the knife blades gauge looked like a buried Buick speedometer needle that had tried to hit 200 mph. We passed into the room. The minor demons had lined up on either side of the entrance and they were clapping and nodding appreciatively. Each wore a jacket with the letters GDHD across the front. I remembered like yesterday the operative I had sold my soul to in that alley, but that was the only one I had ever seen before. Here there were thousands, all clapping heartily. One of them even winked at me.

A voiced boomed from further inside the cavernous chamber. "Come in, come in, our victorious Team Brimstone!"

I looked and saw a smiling LPOD waving us forward. He was flanked by Pazuzu on his left and Melchom on his right,

standing as tall as he could. A number of other major demons
were also in the chamber. I recognized Lamashtu, the Hag
demon. There was no way you could miss those ears and those
long, nasty, curvy nails. I had run into her once before, and
the experience was not pleasant. Because I really don't want
to relive that one, all I'll say is that it involved a torture she
called the Manticore Manicure. Some people should absolutely
not have pets. She saw me looking her way and waved, her
nails swaying. My soul shuddered.

"You have provided my demons and me with exceptional
entertainment value and made some terrific inroads for the
demons of the GDHD, Team Brimstone!" LPOD began. "And
in the process, you shattered the previous *Jingle Hell* points
record. You should all be exceptionally proud! You received
915 sullied soul points!" He pumped his fist in the air and all
of the demons, roared, screeched and hissed. I looked up at the
Evilometer and now noticed the number 915 displayed in old,
Gothic numbers next to a double-lightning-bolt-ish SS.

"And one of you—Simone, please take a step forward—set
an all-time individual record!" The demons made even more
noise. Pazuzu flapped his wings. I thought he almost looked
proud of us. Simone smiled broadly and bowed her head. Pirate
kept turning his head this way and that, shaking his black-
ribbon-bedecked hair.

"Perhaps at no time of the year do more people in one place
seal their ticket to Hell than on Black Friday in the good ol' US
of A," LPOD said. "But your work was truly auspicious, Simone.
How in the world did you get those people worked into such
hatred and loathing over things like off-brand earbuds?"

Simone just smiled prettily and looked down at the floor.

LAMASHTU

Mesopotamian moms lived in fear of Lamashtu. This female demon harassed them during childbirth and tried to kidnap their babies while they were breastfeeding. The name Lamashtu is Akkadian. It means "she who erases."

The home-wrecker is hairy and sports the head of a lioness while also having an asinine appearance due to donkey teeth and ears. Completing the picture are talons in lieu of feet, and extraordinarily long fingers and fingernails.

Although Pazuzu was certainly no party, mothers loved to have him around because he and Lamashtu have never gotten along. In fact, in what might seem odd duty for a demon, Pazuzu was invoked to protect birthing mothers and infants against Lamashtu's malevolence, usually through the use of amulets and statues.

Aliases

****

Abilities

****

Lamashtu can:

‡

Sneak up on almost anyone

‡

Disturb the sleep of both humans and souls

‡

Shoplift like Lindsay, Britney, and Winona

‡

Scratch and bite with the best of them

‡

Kill foliage with a glance

‡

Foul rivers and lakes

‡

Bring disease, sickness, and death

****

"Truly amazing," LPOD continued. "In addition, special recognition is also due Laverne—er, I should say *Dirk*—for the musical addition to this year's show. As I'm sure you will all agree, his "Devil Went Down to Georgia" remake deserved to be made years ago, but Dirk finally turned that annoying, shitty ditty into something with an air of truth and honesty to it! Extra snow cones, ice cream and cold showers—or whatever the Hell we are bestowing as prizes this year—for Dirk!" The demons roared, screeched, and hissed again—and this time some solid snorts were thrown in for good measure.

Just then, LPOD began to look annoyed and particularly evil again.

"Alright, we've had our evil fun. Now everyone, get back to it. SHOW'S OVER," he roared. And with that, the security demons escorted our team back to our cells.

CHAPTER 12

COOLER

Our team never got to see the record-breaking performance, of course. But after we returned, I noticed I was getting a lot more respect from the demons. I also got cold showers (well, sort of lukewarm), chocolate ice cream (the closest thing to black they could find, I guess) and black cherry snow cones. And one day it wasn't just ice cream they dropped off. It was a pint of dark chocolate frozen custard that—according to the pint container—the demons had somehow snagged from Stan's Custard in Milwaukee, Wisconsin. I pictured some shady GDHD operative sidling up to the counter to place his order.

I happened to know the place. The workers there all looked like they had stepped out of the 50s. They sported white pants and white button-up shirts. They even wore little white paper hats. Heavenly attire, of course, which made sense if you happened to like custard as much as I do. But the most amazing thing was who delivered it.

I was sitting in my dark, hot cell trying to picture myself on a tropical beach feeling cool ocean breezes wafting over me when I heard an oddly familiar sound from outside the door. It was the unmistakable trundling noise of a cooler with knobbly wheels being pulled over a hard surface. I jumped up excitedly and waited to see if it stopped outside of my door. It did. The key turned and, incredibly, in rolled Sticks with a plastic Koolman cooler that had clearly been spray painted black.

I was dumbfounded.

"Sticks! I can't believe you're in my cell. Why in Hell are you here?"

He grinned that winning smile of his, looked back over his shoulder to the door and said to the surly demon hovering there, "You'd better get back. I'm going to open this sucker."

The demon shuffled back into the darkness, sneering and looking self-conscious.

Sticks grinned at me, threw open the cooler with a flourish and said, "Special delivery! It's *chocolate custard*!"

"Wow. I love custard. I mean, a lot! That's great, Sticks, but why in the world did they let you deliver it?"

"This guy behind me really, really, really doesn't like cold things," Sticks said with a smile. "He doesn't even like touching this cooler, much less handing out the goods."

He waved the pint toward the demon as if we were going to toss it to him, and he jerked his head back, then snarled. "So because I was the first one on his rounds today, he told me I had to deliver all of these to the team. It's been so incredibly great being able to say hi to everyone. Well, not Floris. I still haven't gotten to him yet."

He dropped his voice down to a whisper.

"And as you can see, when Demon Dan over there gets a little antsy about my chitty chatting too much, I just wave a pint or two his way and he chills out for a bit. I'm sure I'll be tortured after I deliver the last one, but I'm having a blast. I'm a natural-born sales guy, so not being able to talk with folks is one of my greatest punishments down here."

"This is incredible," I said. "No human soul has ever been in my cell before this."

"I know. It's been amazing. So what's up? How've you been?" Sticks grinned at me like we had just met at a neighborhood bar.

"Well, you know," I said. "Not much. Same old same old, I guess. Ah, the other day I did experience a torture that involved being chased through a maze of tunnels by giant, toothy worms. Ick, I hate worms. But of course, they know that."

"Yeah, their ability to tailor our tortures is really something," said Sticks. "My latest involved an excruciating hot wax 'bro-zillian.' It still stings south of my equator." He smiled and waggled a pint at the demon in the hall, then threw it back into the cooler and slammed the lid.

"But what about you?" I asked. "And what do you hear from the others?"

"Well, I did learn that Pirate and Genghis still haven't gotten used to cold deserts. It was pretty hilarious watching them both taste the stuff. Genghis' eyes practically bugged out of his head, and Pirate handled the stuff like it was radioactive. It reminded me of taking some of my colleagues out to eat sushi in Tokyo after we closed a big real estate deal. The itamae—the sushi chef—would take the fish out of the tank and slice them up in front of us. The stuff was still quivering when it hit the plate."

I made a face. "Sounds like something that would happen down here."

"Simone asked about you," Sticks said winking. "She wanted me to say hello. Then she told me about this concept of 'freedom through captivity.' She said she saw this guy who used to be in prison talk about it once. He said that some of the most centered, peaceful, intellectual people he'd ever met are lifers in penitentiaries. I guess there is some doing-time trick that dates back to Confucius, and it leads to enlightenment."

"What's the trick?" I asked.

"She said something about how nobody can imprison your mind if you don't allow it. We are all free to think and feel exactly how we choose. Choose wisely, grasshopper."

"That sounds a little new agey for someone doing time in Hell," I said. "But she is really something. Thinking along those lines down here. That's pretty amazing."

"You speak the truth, Laverne," said Sticks. He laughed and said, "Hey, it was INCREDIBLE seeing you, but I'd better get rolling if I don't want to push my luck too far with Demon Dan. And I do unfortunately still have to drop off a pint to Floris."

"It was great seeing you, too, Sticks." I grabbed the spoon from him, smiled and said, "Thanks so much, guy. See you next Black Friday."

Sticks smiled, turned to leave and bellowed, "On to the next stop, my good man!" He rolled the cooler out of my cell and the door slammed. I heard him rumbling down the aisle and missed him immediately.

It only happened once. Never again did one of my team show up at my cell. But then, one day not long after, a security demon dropped off something that lifted my spirits even higher.

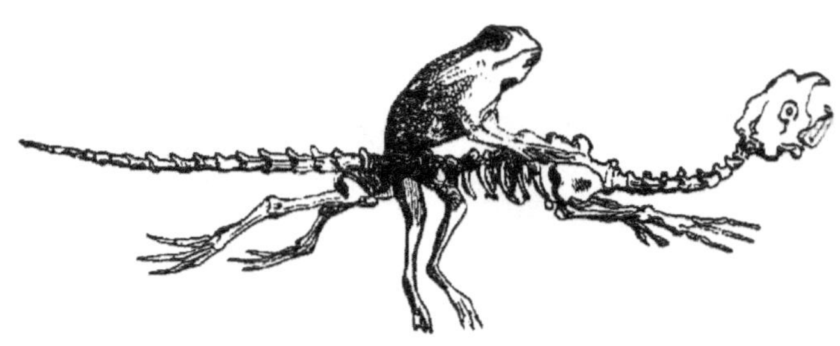

CHAPTER 13

SURPRISE

One day when Hell was just Hell and there were no snow cones or frozen custards in my miserable existence, a security demon came by and dropped off something that completely changed things for me.

I was certainly not an expert and I couldn't get online to check what manufacturing year matched the serial number, but it appeared to me to be a 50s-era Fender Stratocaster with a beaten-up black body, black pickguard and an inky, incredibly smooth ebony fretboard. It had plenty of buckle rash—that is, the finish was worn through pretty well on the back where players had banged the guitar on their belt buckles.

It wasn't my Schecter, but it was a guitar, and a Great One at that. I was absolutely flabbergasted. I felt unworthy. It was like being in jail and having someone deliver a chocolate fountain and fresh fruit, and then after eating your fill be offered a snifter of cognac and a Cuban. It arrived in a dirty old tweed hard case that included extra strings, a wire cutter, some Fender tortoise-shell picks, and a nice (of course black) leather shoulder strap. I had spent about an hour noodling on it when the door burst open and LPOD strode in. He had never been in my cell before, and he had to duck in order to enter.

"Dirk! I just popped by to see if you liked my little gift!"

I didn't even know what to say. LPOD was asking me if I liked his prezzie, and it was the nicest guitar I had ever laid my hands on.

"Wow. Absolutely, LPOD. I've never played such an incredible instrument! Thank you very, very much," I said, looking down. I was truly overawed. Never in my life had anyone given me anything like that.

But wait a minute, I thought. Maybe this was going to be one of those devious Hellish punishments. The guitar would burst into flames in my hands, the strings would melt and burn my fingers, or the guitar's neck would turn into a snake and bite me in the face and I would have an oozing cheek wound for the next century or two. Maybe the shoulder strap would slowly wind around my neck and then jerk me up into the air like a macabre rag doll. What if this was really just the beginning of the cruelest of all the punishments I had ever received in H-E double toothpicks?

But if it wasn't a punishment and I could keep it, I really, really wanted an amp. What good was an incredible electric guitar like this if you couldn't play it through a great amp? But I was pretty sure LPOD wouldn't want anyone else to be able to hear my playing, and an amp would most certainly project the music beyond my cell door. Playing unplugged would probably not be noticed by anyone, even those in the cells on either side of me. But maybe LPOD could create a magical sound barrier? Could I dare to ask? No, I must resist normal temptation to maneuver and connive to get something else this time. I didn't want to screw this up.

"Well, you did such a great job on 'The Devil Went Down to Georgia' without an instrument that I thought you would be able to really knock it out of the park on a new assignment if you actually had a guitar," Satan said.

"I'm very grateful! This is 100 times better than the snow cones and custard. Er, not that I didn't appreciate those. What's the assignment, LPOD?" I asked. "I'm happy to help with anything, of course. It is such an honor to serve you."

"Dirk, this is important. I've decided that our mega-hit show *Jingle Hell* needs a theme song. Something that we can play at the beginning and the end of the show each year that really zings things up a bit. I don't have the faintest idea of what exactly I'm looking for, but I'm pretty sure that with your background you will nail it for me, Dirk. And of course, as a bit of an incentive, as soon as you get something together that works, there will be continued special privileges for you. But be careful, Dirk. I really need your best work on this. If I hate it, there will most certainly be Hell to pay! That's not a joke, by the way." LPOD stared at me malevolently.

I suddenly felt like the guitar had become a trap. If I couldn't please The Most Evil One Himself with a theme song, I would be doomed to even worse suffering than I could imagine. But then again, LPOD had liked my latest creation. *Jingle Hell* needed a theme song, and .... All of a sudden, I knew what it had to be.

"What do you think of working with 'Jingle Bells' itself, LPOD?" I said. "I can give it a really evil, awesome, metal twist with some wailing guitar lines and a solo that will make your demons roar! And I'll write some sick lyrics. You know I can handle lyrics. What do you think?"

LPOD nodded slowly, letting the idea sink in a bit.

"Well, it can't sound anything at all like those insipid versions you hear topside," said LPOD. "If you come up with something that isn't truly evil, I will have you flayed three times a day for the next millennia."

I cringed. Maybe doing regular old hard time like everyone else might be a tad smarter than trying to be Satan's songwriter.

"Of course," I said. "It'll be the most evil incarnation of that Christmas song you've ever heard. Don't worry, LPOD, you're going to love it."

"I'd better, Dirk. When you're ready to record I've got some old analog recording equipment down here somewhere. We'll go for that vintage sound, don't you think?"

"Yes, LPOD," I answered. "That's a great idea. After all, we will be cutting a classic."

LPOD laughed evilly and deeply. "Dirk, I can't wait. Just let your daily punishment demons know when you're ready to record. Now I must be off!"

And with that, Satan levitated out of the cell.

I began to think furiously of how to pull this thing off.

I was usually the king of shortcuts. I realized that my whole life had been made up of them. But this time I was going to have to pull out all of the stops and really work on this. And in the meantime, I had an unbelievably cool, blacked-out ax to play.

CHAPTER 14

27

Now I happen to like all-black guitars. But it is generally more common for black strats to come with white pickguards and white tone and volume knobs. Eric Clapton's Blackie is a great example. But this one was *all* black. Body, fretboard, neck, knobs, pickguard.

It was while getting to know that guitar that I first started thinking about something. White does not exist in Hell. At all. It is certainly dark, but that's not it. Even the eyes of the souls have no whites. They are a sullen grey color.

I guess it make sense. In Heaven, I'm sure everyone is flapping around on white gossamer wings and taking strolls on clouds. Everyone must also have perfectly white teeth. Their plain white T's never need bleaching. The unicorns are BRILLIANT white, of course, and they poop sparkly white whipped cream along with those rainbows.

That reminds me. Some idiot once told me that Janis Joplin, Jim Morrison, and Jimi Hendrix all had a white Bic lighter in their pocket when they died at age 27. I fell for it, of course, and told the story to a load of people before I learned the truth. Janis was found wearing a short, pocketless nightgown, and Morrison (we think) died nude in the bathtub of his Paris apartment. If he was carrying a lighter, it must have been rather uncomfortable. Then you find out that the Bic lighter wasn't introduced until 1973. All three of those cats died before that.

Funny, right? But the other part of that myth does have a creepy side to it. Robert Johnson—one of the biggest blues guys ever—died in 1938, also at the age of 27. And by the way, many people thought he had cut a deal with LPOD. Kurt Cobain booked his ride on the ultimate pain train when he was 27. One month after his mates kicked him out of the Rolling Stones, founding member Brian Jones took his last dive into that swimming pool at his English country home at the same age. The year after Canned Heat played at Woodstock, 27-year-old guitarist Al "Blind Owl" Wilson—who had a strange habit of sleeping outdoors—was found in his bandmate's yard with his hands crossed over his chest and a bottle of barbiturates at his side. Ron "Pigpen" McKernan, the original frontman of the Grateful Dead, is a member of the 27 Club. As is Pete Ham of Badfinger, who joined just three days away from his 28th birthday. There was Amy Winehouse in her London home in 2011. And Dave Alexander, bassist for the Stooges. Jean-Michel Basquiat, an artist and Andy Warhol buddy who also founded the band Gray. D. Boon, guitarist and lead singer of the punk band Minutemen. Kristen Pfaff, bassist for Hole and friend of Cobain—two months after Cobain passed.

So many great talents and the number 27. Wikipedia lists 56 of them last time I looked—check it out.

Creeped out yet? One more for you.

CHAPTER 15

FANBASE

I worked and worked on that song. Well, for a while I did. What else did I have to do but experience either pain and agony, or crushing boredom while roasting like a rotisserie chicken in my cell? Frankly, the work took my mind off of the daily dose of torture and allowed a tiny space of my soul to experience things that I hadn't experienced for a while. To have music in one's existence, I realized, was more important than I had ever realized. Perhaps one of my greatest punishments was having to leave it behind.

So as music re-entered my soul, so did thoughts one didn't generally have in Hell. Sort of—ah, I guess there is no way around this—*nice* thoughts. Looking back on things, I realized that the music probably impacted me more than I imagined.

My work for LPOD suffered, though, when some security demons began taking me to an isolated cavern and to play some songs for them. No amp, of course, but it was awfully quiet in Hell when you got away from the screaming masses. So it was in those caverns that I got dozens of demons tapping their talons to songs like "Hells Bells," "Highway to Hell,"

"Black Dog"—they absolutely loved AC/DC and Led Zeppelin—
and then even some of my own Glütenfreake hits such as
"Ace of Hades," "Prayer of the Python," "Throttle Me," and
"Lipstick Poison." I really had them guffawing over a sappy yet
brutal James Taylor knock off called "You've Got a Fiend." The
demons loved it. Heck, they loved me! Other than when they
were torturing souls, never before had I seen them having so
much fun.

So my existence in Hell was taking a turn for the better.
But all of this performing did take a toll on my songwriting,
so when the next Black Friday was just over the horizon, the
theme song wasn't yet ready. Which was, of course, really NOT
a good thing.

CHAPTER 16

GRILL

"Whad'ya mean you were *DISTRACTED*!" LPOD roared so ferociously that the lava pool in the torture chamber sloshed as if it was hit by a Category 5 hurricane. He pointed at Pazuzu, who was manning the temperature control on the industrial cooking range I was stretched across. Each time he pointed at his demon helper, the flames licked up the sides of me with their burning tongues and I couldn't help screaming out in agony.

Despite the extreme pain, I had enough presence of mind to know how incredibly stupid it would be to implicate any of the demons who had kept asking me to perform what they had begun to call *The Best Hits of Hell Show*. And Pazuzu had become one of my biggest fans, which was also unfortunate because he kept breaking wind during the performances and it was way too easy to hear because I still didn't have an amp. Also, even though Pazuzu was the one who was being directed by Satan to flame broil me, I simply couldn't turn in my fans. So all I said was "Yeeeeeooooow! I am soooooo sorry. Give me another chance! Please, Your Most Supremely Powerful King of Darkness! I promise I will get it done for you!"

"You're making me look bad, Laverne," said Satan. "I had confidence in you, so I made the mistake of telling some demons in the production department that we would have a theme song for this year's show. I DON'T LIKE TO LOOK BAD, LAVERNE. PEOPLE HAVE BEEN MAKING ME LOOK BAD FOR A REALLY (point) REALLY (point) REALLY (point) LONG TIME! The flames flickered up my side as Pazuzu repeatedly cranked up the heat on demand, though it seemed as though he might be letting the fire go down lower than usual in between Satan's exhortations. A true fan, to be sure.

"You have one more chance, Laverne. THAT'S IT!" boomed LPOD. "DON'T MAKE ME LOOK BAD AGAIN, LAVERNE! I'VE GOT SOME SEGWAYS DOWN HERE WITH YOUR NAME ON THEM, AND THIS TIME YOU'RE GOING TO WISH IT WAS JUST AN EXPRESSWAY YOU FELL INTO!"

CHAPTER 17

BLACK

I fondly remember my black phase. Well, my first black phase.

When I was a senior in high school, just as I was really getting into music, I started wearing only black. Black jeans, black shirts, black socks, black shoes, black belt. Even black underwear. I shit you not.

It made me feel like a real rocker. But it went beyond that. I can't really tell you exactly, but it sort of made me feel protected. It was like a superhero shield—a protective, super-hardened, Ironman-like titanium suit that didn't allow anything to touch me emotionally. Any high school kid can tell you why something like that is important. Go ahead and ask them.

Wearing black works on all ages, too. The youngsters give you some room. Depending on your choice of duds, older folks think you might be a priest or minister so they also generally give you a wide berth. It's not like going Goth and it doesn't require piercings or tats (I got those later), so the parents are actually sort of OK with it.

The drawbacks? Well, it's awfully hot in summer. To make matters worse in that season, short-sleeved black shirts just don't feel like the thing. So a very effective deodorant is a must for anyone dressing hot by dressing black. Also, depending on wardrobe choice the possibility of being ID'd as a priest has to have a bit of a chilling effect on women.

Another advantage is simplicity, of course. You never have to think too much about what to wear. Stains are almost never noticeable. Doing laundry is a breeze.

Shopping is also simplified, and you find that you really don't need that many clothes. Just enough to not have to do the laundry so often. And that, of course, means that there aren't many all-black clothing people at Black Friday sales. But Hell is full of them. We're all dressed to depress down here. Again, it has something to do with the color scheme or the overall gloom or something. Even things that aren't black look black, or a really dark gray.

You might also be wondering how "Black Friday" got its name. Is there some sinister story behind the moniker, or is it something as benign as my choice of wardrobe? Well, I read an article about it once and learned that some say black was used because it was the single day on the calendar when most retailers finally generated a profit on the year. They weren't in the red any longer—they were in the black. I think this story gets a lot of airplay with the retailers because they want you to think they have been trudging through the business desert, trying to break even for the whole long year and then— finally—the oasis of Black Friday comes into view. We are SAVED! That, of course, just hides the fact they've been getting filthy rich all year long.

The true story behind Black Friday, however, is just a tad darker. In the 50s, Philly cops used the term to describe the craziness that took place the day after Thanksgiving when herds of shoppers and tourists swarmed into the city before the big Army-Navy game that took place that Saturday. Instead of having time with their families and lying around in a tryptophan fuzz, Philly cops would have to work extra-long shifts dealing with the crowds and traffic. Shoplifters and pickpockets would have a field day in all of the chaos, adding to the cops' pain. By the 60s, Philly merchants tried to change the term to "Big Friday" in order to polish up the day's image a bit.

Then in the 80s retailers figured out a way to recast Black Friday and spin it into something that seemed a bit more "positive." Ergo, the idea that the day after Thanksgiving, America's stores finally turned a profit. That Black Friday story stuck, and pretty soon most people forgot about the Philly experience.

Although I do hear that Philly football fans treat visiting football fans pretty hellishly.

CHAPTER 18

ELECTRIC

Before I knew it, Black Friday was upon us again, and we were in the plane. We were excited, ready to roll, ready to sully souls by the truckload. I turned to Pirate and said, "Magnifique, eh?" (That was about the extent of my French.) He loved that. He ran off for about a minute with some goofy French gobbledygook, and I just kept nodding and smiling. When he wound down and took a breath, I gave him a thumbs up and, smiling, turned to Simone.

"Know any French, by chance?" I asked. Simone said, "No, I know some Mandarin and I'm passably fluent in Spanish. No French, though. Having said that, it certainly seems to me that he likes you." I turned back to Pirate, who was sporting a grin that reminded me of a hockey player due to the fact that 50 percent of his teeth were missing.

"Magnifique, eh?" I said again. Pirate slapped me on the back. Simone let out a cute little snort as she tried not to laugh.

This year's playing field for Team Brimstone was right up Simone's alley: we were headed to Electric Alley, the largest electronics chain in the United States. With Simone's knowledge of the industry, I was absolutely convinced a new record was within our reach. She had given us all some ideas as to what product areas were generally in shortest supply. Spirits were high and were about to get higher as I looked up and heard those noises in the ceiling of the plane again. Then ... *w h o o s h !*

Before I knew it, I was passing through the legs of some rather large Electric Alley employee who was evacuating his bowels prior to facing the Black Friday hordes. My thankfully incorporeal soul shuddered, and I staggered through the door of the men's room and into the front of the store.

The employees, all clad in the obligatory blue and orange motley of the Electric Alley employee, were rushing around excitedly. Everybody seemed ready for action, their wireless radio earpieces squawking with last-minute instructions. The atmosphere of the store crackled with a kind of human-fired electricity.

I watched as the keepers of the keys ceremoniously opened the doors. I realized that their clocks must be running a little late, as I could see some customers outside the store pointing at their watches or cell phone clocks. All the better for Team Brimstone!

It had been twelve long human months since I had last heard it, but it excited me to no end to once again hear the excited rush of the horde. It was so primal. The hunt was on. The competition between humans to see what spoils they could drop or drag down in the hunting grounds had begun. Adrenaline pulsed. Sweat flowed. Souls were about to be sullied.

I immediately swung into action. There was no hesitation this time. I headed to the small appliances area where a mob was trying to get their hands on deeply discounted PowerBlast Blenders. As soon as I swooped into that area, I particularly preyed upon those who were hangry and therefore managed to quickly tally beaucoup SS points. The mixture of limited quantities of blenders and limited blood sugar levels proved exceptionally potent.

After noticing some mild pushing near the stand mixers, I moved in to ratchet up the fun, deciding to encourage petty larceny. I whispered to one woman, "If you don't get that last buttermilk-colored mixer—yes, the one in the hands of that crazy old hag there—you will NEVER find another one that will fit your decor. She doesn't care. Just take it from her basket when her back is turned." As the first woman sidled up and lifted the box out, the second turned around and saw the robbery in progress. A quick whisper to the other woman from me and the catfight was on. Cursing, screaming, clawing, and biting ensued. I chuckled to myself, thinking that it all kind of sounded like a fairly quiet day in Hell. Then I saw that I had just gotten double points for creating the first fight of the morning. This was a new scoring enhancement that had been put in place for this year's competition.

Out of the corner of my eye, I saw Sticks making hay in home computers. It started with some modest shoving, but soon evolved into a heavy-duty mosh pit scene. Actually, calling it a mosh pit didn't do justice to the level of violence that ensued. One man clamshelled a laptop onto another man's head, squeezing away until I heard a loud crack. I thought it was the laptop screen, but I wasn't exactly sure.

Pirate headed toward the home theater area, but almost seemed overwhelmed by the technology and noise there. He then set up a base of operations in mobile phones, where he was clearly creating chaos and racking up points. His maniacal grin revealed his dental shortcomings. Lord knows what he was whispering to the shoppers, I thought to myself. What in the world could a Pirate know that would help him sully souls in a mobile phone department?

I couldn't see Simone, but I did see Floris. Not surprisingly, he was in the video game area. As he floated and flitted from one mark to another, he lowered his head and looked utterly ruthless.

A couple of hours later, the store was already in complete shambles. That was when I saw Simone. The demons were going to *love* this. She had just gotten a cop to taser the store manager, who was lying on the ground jerking around piteously. Several of his employees were looking down at him and laughing.

I thought I had seen it all when I noticed that over in the area with the tablet computers, two women were slamming their carts into each other while one of them had a four- or five-year-old kid in the cart's child seat. The little guy's head was violently jerking back and forth, yet the women continued their demo derby dustup. Some people need to head to Hell just a little bit sooner than the rest of us.

The fun was still going strong when the timer hit 6:06:06. The major appliances department was just heating up then, as was wearable technologies. Unfortunately, the subterranean suck began. I passed through the men's restroom door and into a (thankfully) empty stall, and then began my travel back to my own personal Hell.

CHAPTER 19

REPEAT

This time the celebration was over the top, particularly for the Underworld. I had never seen so many GDHD agents in one cavern before. They were cheering wildly as our team entered. LPOD was hovering in the air, pointing at the Evilometer gauge with his pitchfork and clicking his hind hoofs together. Someone had even turned up the temperature of the lava pool and it bubbled away happily.

"Team Brimstone are winners again!" he boomed. And with a score of 999 you have set another record!" In a sing-songy voice, he then added, "And what is really great is that 999 makes 666 if you turn it upside down! Hello! How cool is THAT?"

Many of the demons looked at each other as if they had never heard of anything as witty or wise, nodding solemnly and snorting. Others just looked confused and craned their necks so that they could see what LPOD was talking about.

"Our entire cadre of off-duty GDHD agents are here today, Team Brimstone, because you have just made their work easier than ever before," LPOD said. They have A LOT of souls to follow up on in the coming weeks and months. Never before have we seen a score like that, and never before have we had a team win *Jingle Hell* two years running! This is truly an auspicious event! Let's give this team our absolute finest Hell Yell, demons!"

Satan stretched his arms in the air, the pitchfork in one hand and the hook'em horns showing in the other, and he opened his evil pie hole wide and bellowed his best into the stalactites. With that, the screams, wails, and roaring began. It was so loud that the Evilometer appeared to be shaking. I should also note that the fumes coming out of those throats were also enough to take paint off a Porsche.

After what seemed like hours, the din subsided and the demons slumped where they stood.

"OK, OK. Show's over, everybody. Get back to work!" LPOD shouted. "I can't WAIT for next year! But Dirk—come over here."

I shuffled over in a way that I hoped seemed sufficiently fawning.

"How's that theme song coming along? You've had plenty of time, fella. You BETTER not let me down. I'm keeping those Segways charged and ready for you ..."

It just wasn't ready yet. Some of the lyrics sounded ridiculous, and the guitar solo was weak. But I had learned a long time ago not to make The James Bond Mistake. Some arch idiot always thinks the game is over, so they spill all of the beans to Bond and then 007 of course escapes and knows *exactly* what is happening, even though he had no *friggin* idea until that very moment. I knew to keep things quiet until I was absolutely sure I knew things were in hand. No need to tell much right now. LPOD might even ask me to perform the song in its current form, and that could result in months of pain, I was sure.

"Don't you worry, LPOD. You'll have your theme song," I said. "And you're going to love it so much you're going to want it on continuous repeat as you sharpen your fangs every morning." (Was that a tad too familiar to say to LPOD?

I panicked for a moment.) "It certainly does get the day off to a strong start when you begin it with some awesome evil metal music, don't ya think?" I saw the volcanic expression on Satan's face and immediately looked down meekly.

"I don't sharpen my teeth every morning, you idiot," bellowed LPOD. "But you better DELIVER, or I will ask my demons NOT to sharpen some things that will be used on *YOU.*"

With that, LPOD levitated out of the chamber without looking back.

CHAPTER 20

CHAMP

LPOD must have found out. The elicit cavern concerts stopped completely, and—sadly—I was pretty much left alone except for the usual punishments and prize deliveries. Snow cones and custard arrived intermittently, and one day I had a lukewarm shower. (Yeah, it wasn't even really cold. Cheap.) And one time I was also treated to a serving of Baked Alaska, which was fantastic but the meringue was way too dark. I couldn't blame anyone, though. Keeping any heat and/or flames under control in Hell is a losing battle.

After an indeterminable period of time, one of the demons made another delivery that really made my millennium. It was an old, dirty, beat up little Fender Tweed Champ amp with a black, braided guitar cable and a pair of over-the-ear headphones. I couldn't believe it! I plugged the Champ into the wall socket that was generally only used for electrical torture instruments, slid the cable into both the guitar and the amp, put on the cans and toggled on the power.

The tone was incredible. I turned it up to about three and dug in. That's where Champs begin to distort. Angels

sing, but so do electric guitars. I remembered the first time
I played through an amp. It was the same kind of magical,
inspirational, uplifting, gorgeous, striking, soothing, pleading,
loving tone. Power chords roared, solos wailed and soared.

As the tones reverberated through my soul, I suspected that
my Hell-cell had just become the best gig in the neighborhood.
After playing through the amp for a couple of blissful minutes, I
noticed something. There was an ancient-looking tag hanging
off the handle of the Champ. It was the kind of manila paper
label with a red rimmed string hole that they would put on
equipment at a guitar and amp repair shop. I looked at it
closely. On one side it had a name, date, and claim number.
Pete Bell, February 27, 1953, #7347. I flipped over the label.
In startling red ink, an antique-looking scrawl said, "You're
running out of time, Laverne."

The amp—which I found out later could only create sound
through the headphones—had provided just the catalyst I
needed. I was done in no time. And the theme song was,
even in my generally not-so-humble opinion, *awesome*. I also
cranked out some pretty bad ass metal-ish versions of some
other Christmas classics, including "Deck the Hell" (I loved
the part with, "Don we now our demon apparel"), "Hark the
Herald Demons Sing," "We Wish You a Crappy Christmas (and
a Hellish New Year)" and "Carol of the Hell Cells." I was on a
roll and really getting into the spirit of things.

CHAPTER 21

STUDIO

I recorded the *Jingle Hell* theme song in a studio cavern miles and miles away from the general cell blocks. A huge, super-thick, iron and rubber door festooned with two large, rusting "Recording in Progress" signs in Gothic script sealed the cavern to prevent sound leakage. As is the case with many recording studios I have had the pleasure of visiting, the room was filled with acoustical foams, fabric wrapped panels, and sound diffusers.

Although I had brought the little Fender Champ along, it wasn't necessary. The place was stacked with some of the best amps in the world. The whole setup was world class. I'd never seen anything like it before.

And LPOD was right about the analog sound board. It was old and massive—a true relic. The Beatles might have recorded through it. The studio demons were efficient and oddly courteous. No bellowing or screaming, just polite exchanges with everybody, including me.

MURMUX

With no fewer than thirty
legions at his disposal, Murmux
is both a Great Duke and an Earl
of Hell. He is known as the demon
of music. Before the Fall, he was
called Matthias and was a member
of the Order of Thrones. Also called
the Ophanim, the Order of the
Thrones is the highest-level order
of angelic hierarchy. Renowned
for their wisdom, they never sleep
because they are constantly busy
guarding God's throne. They are all
highly caffeinated.

Murmux is often shown
wearing soldier's garb and a
crown. His mode of transport is
generally either griffin or vulture.
When he is really trying to make
an impression, two of his mini
ministers go before him blowing
trumpets.

Murmux is one of the three
demons that hold sway over the
dead. Murmux takes over the souls,
while Bune and Bifrons are in
charge of corpses.

ALIASES

****

Murmur
Murmus

ABILITIES

****

Murmux can:
⁜
Remain perpetually vigilant
⁜
Hear with extreme precision
⁜
*Beat almost anyone at
"Name that Tune"*
⁜
*Force souls to answer questions
posed by a conjurer*

****

I had been in a couple of oddball (low-cost) studios before
up top, and they were generally filled with quirky and often
addled looking studio techs, engineers, and runners, the latter
being the youngest, lowliest engineers who got everyone
sandwiches and made sure the alcohol delivery was made
without a hitch. But here, the glowing meters on the board
illuminated a serious bunch of demons who were intently
going about their work. How incredibly odd it was, I thought,
that I was so settled in down here that I now saw some demons
as less quirky than humans.

The funny things about these demons, though, was that
they were all of the smaller variety. That puzzled me for a
minute, but then it dawned on me. It was the all-hands team.
Larger demons would not have been able to efficiently work
the board controls due to their massive meat hooks.

And then the producer arrived. He seemed to emerge from
the very earth itself, riding a very large, ratty tatty looking
vulture. One minute he wasn't there, and the next he was.
He swung his leg over the vulture and dismounted like John
Wayne jumping off a Hollywood nag. Towering over the
other demons on the board, he wore both a crown and a black
hoodie. The hood was up so it was very hard to see his face,
but the red eyes were visible. He also wore black jeans and
blacked-out Vans.

"I AM MURMUX," the demon announced. "Great Duke and
Earl of Hell, I am the music demon."

And I am not impressed, I thought. For a demon, this guy
was pretty unimposing. I mean, really—a hoodie? This was the
first demon I had met who, other than those pretty boss skids,
looked like he had wardrobed up at Shopmart.

"Let's get the guitar part first," Murmux said.

It didn't take me too long to become grudgingly impressed
with that guy. I could tell Murmux was a great producer.
Although I was convinced that the first take was all that was
needed, Murmux pushed harder. After two takes, he personally
adjusted the microphone placement. The demon even took
over the soundboard at one point. His directions to the other

demons were curt and quiet. His voice was melodic and strangely soft. I never once saw his entire face. But those eyes were as intense as laser gun sights.

When Murmux called it a wrap, I was even more convinced that we had recorded a hit. And then the sound demons completely blindsided me by giving me some pretty dangerous high fives. (Lots of claws.) Murmux just nodded. But then it occurred to me. Didn't I still need to lay down the vocals?

Just then I heard a deep, resonant rumbling outside of the door to the studio. I had never heard anything like it in Hell, but it reminded me of being in an underground Chicago "L" station when a train emerged through a tunnel. An engineer demon ran over and swung the double doors open.

Outside was the largest demon I had ever seen. He looked like some sort of evil elephant with a nasty beer belly. Actually, I had heard of this guy before. Behemoth was his name, and he was said to be one heckuva baritone. I had once heard him singing a really creepy sort of demon fight song once when I was spending some time relaxing on a bed of nails.

"Welcome, Behemoth," said Murmux. "Your timing is impeccable."

"Well, I do have the best rhythm in Hell," said Behemoth. "And YOU," he looked at me, "must be Laverne. I have not yet had the pleasure of making you suffer, have I?"

"No, Behemoth," I said. "But I will of course look forward to it."

"I'm sure you will," Behemoth said, scowling and looking away dismissively. He then brightened and turned back to Murmux. "So you are ready for me?"

"Yes," said Murmux, softly. "I know you like to gargle and sing some scales, so why don't you go ahead and do that. We will begin as soon as you are ready." He then turned to me and said, "You may go."

As an artist, I was of course appalled that I wasn't going to sing. But as I packed up my Strat, I took great consolation in the fact that—after everything I'd been through—I was really beginning to hit it big, albeit it in Hell.

BEHEMOTH

Behemoth is the butler and high cupbearer of Hell. That's a fancy way of saying he oversees LPOD's room service and the catering of the massive feasts and banquets held in Hell. Examples of the latter include the annual, backslapping get-togethers of various legions, and banquets to celebrate particularly evil holidays or terrible events on earth that happen as a result of demonic intercession.

The Dictionnaire Infernal depicts Behemoth as an oddly jolly looking elephant grasping his rotund belly. He has also been depicted as a hippopotamus, rhinoceros, or water buffalo. In an ancient Jewish text called the Book of Enoch, Behemoth is the quintessential monster of the land, whereas Leviathan rules the seas and Ziz the sky. Some accounts say that he originally inhabited an invisible desert east of the Garden of Eden.

Aliases

****

Behemot (modern)

Abilities

****

Behemoth can:

***

Bring to bear extraordinary strength and endurance

***

Sing with the best of them. His size undoubtedly contributes to his deep, oddly melodious (for a demon) baritone. He is considered Hell's official demonic singer

***

Ingest enormous amounts of food (and other unspeakable matter)

***

Induce extreme fear into others, particularly when he invades their personal space

****

JITTERS

The walk back to my cell was like going home right after watching the latest amazing action flick at a theater on Sunday night when you know you have to go to work the next day and your boss is more than a tad crazy. Every step I took brought me a little back into bleak, black reality. I began to ask questions that hadn't occurred to me before. Will I be able to keep the guitar now that the song was cut? Certainly LPOD might need some other songs written? My heart sank. Who was I kidding? I was in Hell, after all. One didn't see a lot of "nice-to-haves" in Hell. I was pretty sure that this guitar I was carrying, now snug in its case, my only joy in this awful place, was soon to be gone. "Gone Daddy Gone," as the Violent Femmes song title put it.

And what happened if the team and I didn't win again this coming year? What were the chances of us pulling off a three-peat? I felt about as hopeful of that as I was of being allowed to keep the guitar, and in a way that felt even worse. I was really going to miss those guys when I couldn't see them once a year. Especially Simone.

I began to get more and more sullen. My feet began to drag. It wasn't fair, damn it. I spent my life doing everything I could to become a star. Sure, I had cut corners, manipulated people and connived my way to the successes I had achieved topside. But I really felt like I had earned my star status down here. How could I go back to being just one soul doing hard time?

Then I stopped dead in my tracks. With Behemoth cutting the vocals on "*Jingle Hell*," LPOD had taken away too much. Sure, I had created the arrangement and written the lyrics, and topside that was where the real money was. Royalty checks were certainly the cat's meow. But given the current realities, I had been manipulated by LPOD into being even more obscure than I had been before. Behemoth would get all the glory.

I once visited my mom's 99-year-old cousin in an old folks home. I brought her a bottle of Jack Daniels because she really like to have a snort every evening. I stayed for about an hour, and as I said my goodbyes, she pointed to same bottle sitting on the counter and said, "See that bottle of my good friend Jack? My friend the maintenance man brought me that. I am so lucky to have Bob in my life!"

The security demon said, "Come on, Laverne, move it! I have a lava pool party to get to!" I walked on, getting more morose by the step.

Was there a silver lining here? (That, of course, isn't the most common thing to find down in Hell, but I always find it is remarkably useful to look for such things.) Generally, of course, any positive answer to that question in Hell tends to involve a pretty heavy layer of tarnish, but every little bit helps.

The only possible silver lining I could see in my future involved me being able to keep the guitar. I would even be OK with losing the amp. Not particularly happy, but OK. Then I thought about when I was making it as a musician in life. If I was truthful with myself, it wasn't so much the little bit of fame I achieved that made me happy. It was the experience of creating something. The experience of creating music. The experience of creating beauty. I really needed that guitar.

But LPOD was going to take it back. I was absolutely sure of it. The feeling was more terrible than a three-month thumbscrew. But things were about to get a lot worse.

CHAPTER 23

SKITTERING

I got back to my cell and the security demon slammed the door shut. I put my guitar and amp in the corner and was just sitting down on the bare iron bed when I thought I heard something skittering about in the shadows above. There was a faint click-clacking sound near both of my ears and then—absolutely terrified and paralyzed with fear now—I felt something strange and sharp brushing my neck. I couldn't move. Suddenly, vicious talons dug into my throat and yanked my head back.

Now, most do assume that one's time in Hell is spent in extraordinary discomfort. Pain and agony are of course standard fare, with a healthy helping of excruciating, ripping, soul-gibbering nightmares that spice things up occasionally. But the part of the program I could never seem to get used to in any way, shape, or form was the way demons liked to sneak up on you and terrify the living crap out of you. You would think it wouldn't be such a big deal, but to me—at least—it was. It REALLY was.

"As someone consigned to the fiery regions, you are having a bit too much fun for my liking," I heard a raspy voice say directly into my ear.

"GEEZ!," I shouted as my soul shuddered and I twisted away and bolted to the other side of the cell. I pawed at my neck with both hands, trying futilely to get rid of the mega heebie jeebies I was feeling. Hanging off the wall like a spider was Lamashtu, the Hag. She skittered down the wall and sat on my bed, glaring at me malevolently. Her eyes were a diseased shade of yellow.

"I wanted to give you a little visit today to let you know that I am watching and waiting, Laverne." She smiled distastefully.

"What are you talking about?" I asked.

"Don't take that tone with me, young man," snarled Lamashtu. "Or I will plug in my electric hair curler and work on your fingers and toes for a month or two." She shook her big, black Prada purse at me. Somehow that seemed to minimize the hair curler threat just a bit. Nevertheless, I knew better than to taunt a demon.

"I'm very sorry," I said, looking down at the floor. "Please go on, most illustrious Lamashtu."

"That's better," she said. Then she caught herself. "But don't think for a moment that fawning will win you any points with me, Laverne. It might work on some of the ego-centric, dimwit demons down here liked Pazuzu, but it just annoys those of us with real brains. Those of us who—frankly—are getting a bit tired of you turning this place into Club Red Resorts. This is NOT a nice cozy vacation spot, for Satan's sake."

I did my best to keep my mouth shut as the hag regarded me with a look that could have curdled milk.

"All I need is for your lousy team to lose this year, and then no one will care about you any longer—YOU WILL BE MINE!" said Lamashtu. "I am going to spend the next millennium or so taking you on the Best Tortures in Hell circuit." She cocked her head and rested her chin on a fist that was bristling with those nasty, curvy, yellowy nails. "Maybe we'll start with a decade or two sitting in the Airplane Economy Class area. It's one of my particular favorites. The suffering there is so excruciatingly delicious!" She cackled loudly and licked her lips excitedly.

I could feel her staring at me, but I did my best to keep my eyes on the floor.

"Your ass is grass, Laverne, and I am a big ol' riding lawn mower with the cutting deck set *low*!" With that she screeched, cackled some more, and left the cell, slamming the door behind her.

CHAPTER 24

BREASTPLATES

Whenever I was trying to take my mind off Lamashtu and everything else, I thought a lot about Simone. When you carried that eternal damnation thing around with you all day, you really needed a bit of a mental coffee break once in a while. So I thought of Simone licking my ear lobe as some imp tightened me up on the rack. She would laugh and say, "Laverne, you are wayyyyy too tight! You need to relax!"

Then I thought of her running ice cubes down my chest and to my belly button. "You're cool, Laverne, but I can make you even cooler!"

Then I would picture her riding a demon dragon and wearing a breastplate and a latex catsuit. She would be driving along the Plain of Sorrows wielding a bullwhip. And I'd look up at her in awe and hope that I could catch her attention—just for a moment. The flames from below would reflect off of her eyes. Ahhhhhh.

As I mentioned, it's not exactly like you get randy down here. But if and when you feel any such sensation, you do know that you are *never* going to be satisfied.

ELIGOS

As a Great Duke of Hell, Eligos commands 60 legions of demons. Eligos easily locates hidden things, and he is particularly fond of plotting and subterfuge. He favors the cunning over the strong. Those who hold high office are particularly susceptible to Eligos.

He takes the form of a knight carrying a lance, an ensign, and a scepter. Aleister Crowley, the famous—yet extremely creepy looking—British occultist, magician, poet, painter, novelist and mountaineer of the late 19th and early 20th century, claimed that Eligos also carried a serpent. When he is feeling particularly dramatic, Eligos can appear as a ghostly specter who rides a winged, semi-skeletal horse. This Steed of Eligos is a minion of Hell itself. It is a reanimated corpse of one of the horses that lived in the Garden of Eden. And yes, it does like to eat apples.

ALIASES

****

Abigor
Eligor
Lord of Intrigue
Lord of Conjuring

ABILITIES

****

Eligos can:
‡
Perceive every intention
‡
Discover hidden things
‡
*Best the IBM Deep Blue
chess-playing computer*
‡
*Ascertain the future outcome
of wars*
‡
*Make self-important people
look very, very silly*

****

CHAPTER 25

CUTS

I suppose it comes as no surprise to anyone that in music you are likely to meet a lot of people with issues. It's probably the same across all sorts of professions, but I do think it has got to be worse in the music business. I had been one of those people. I tended to get stuck in obsession loops. Instead of just letting things happen, I worried about things way too much. Meditation helped a bit, and I also found some useful mind tricks in Buddhist teachings. I remember one Buddhist nun in this audiobook I listened to on my iPhone. In her interesting Tibetan accent, she had said something like, "See yourself as a leafless tree in winter. Let the winter winds blow through your branches."

I was thinking of exactly that as I endured the latest installment of my eternal torture. This one was particularly awful. I called it, "Really Bad Day at the Office." Let's just say it has to do with paper cuts. A LOT of paper cuts. I was whimpering to beat the band when, out of the corner of my consciousness, I saw a swarm of very concerned security demons swing by.

"LPOD is NOT having a fun day," one of the demons
muttered surreptitiously as he scurried past.

"If one of my demons spoke out of line like that, I would
introduce him to my favorite dagger," said my torturer, Eligos.
He grabbed a fresh sheet of paper.

LPOD floated into the torture chamber. He said, "I know
you're having fun right now Eligos, but I need your help on
something. You have done such a great job for me in the past
on the big strategy stuff. For example, those improvements you
put in place on Project 27 have been very effective. You've got
a real flair for this stuff, as you know, and I need some of that
zizzle from you on this one, I'll tell you."

"Thank you very much for saying that, LPOD. How can I
help you today?" Eligos rapidly stroked the edge of the paper
into my left index finger.

"Yieeeeeeeee," I shrieked.

"Nice to see you, too, Laverne," said LPOD. "Now please
be quiet. Eligos, we have a bit of a challenge that I need you
to tackle."

"Sure thing, LPOD."

The two of them walked some distance away, but I could
still make out their conversation.

"You know how much I love our little *Jingle Hell* program.
Well, some nutcase, smoothie-sucking freak who runs an
outdoor sporting goods chain is making trouble for our
Black Friday fun. I'm sure it's nothing more than a gnat on
Nebuchadnezzar, but he's got my dander up and I want him
squashed," said LPOD.

He strode a little further away, his hideous, clawed hands
clasped behind his back, and Eligos followed. LPOD's voice
lowered conspiratorially, but I could still hear him.

"You know how incredible the conversion rate has been
with those we are able to sully through *Jingle Hell*. Well, this
guy, Stewart Shepherd—they apparently call him *STEW*, for
the love of evil—has started something that I want you to put
a stop to before anyone else begins to think it's a good idea.

He's announcing that this year they won't have a Black Friday sale, and that everyone should either *spend time with family, exercise, or just enjoy the great outdoors*. Can you believe it?" LPOD looked horrified.

"I should be exceedingly happy to exercise this Stew at the tip of my lance," said Eligos grimly as he shook the cruel instrument.

"Of course, of course, Eligos. That *would* be fun. Hmmmm. I hadn't thought of that!" He smiled and then shook his head as if to clear the vision from his head. "But what I really want you to do is to infiltrate their board of directors and call this man's sanity into question. We need him out of there. I mean, come on, he's doing his shareholders a terrible disservice. Whoever heard of shutting down on Black Friday!"

"Ridiculous!" said Eligos. "I'll leave immediately." And he did. He mounted his winged steed and they flapped off into the dark distance.

LPOD seemed a little shocked at the abrupt departure. He recovered quickly.

"Right. Nice to have demons you can count on," LPOD said to no one in particular. He levitated off down a hall with his security demons ahead and behind him.

"LPOD's on the move," several of them announced.

I sat there alone, waiting for the inevitable. Then it came, with LPOD booming from down the hall.

"You imbeciles! Take him back to his cell!"

iNSIGHTS

More musings from the Netherworld. I've thought more than once that it would be really incredible to be able to conduct research in Hell. Call it the Soul Poll. A Soul Census would be pretty cool, too. You could do that every 100 years or so. Every 10 seems too quick for such a cosmic county. But a regular Soul Poll would provide the pulse of those without a pulse, the absolute best source of dirt on the damned.

Because resources are relatively unlimited in Hell and everyone has time to burn, we would be able to ask a *lot* of questions. Thousands of them, I suppose. We'd keep some questions the same forever and create new ones as the spirit(s) moved. I always thought it would be great if LPOD let me be in charge. Although I suppose he would put a demon at the helm. Eh, wait a minute. Maybe not. From what I've seen, demons have a tremendous ability to be clueless about human souls.

For example, I was once on a march to a torture area when the particularly horrifying security demon escorting me stopped and said, "Do humans get upset stomachs in the light as we demons do?"

Given that fact, maybe you could sell this idea to LPOD as a tool to help the security demons do their jobs better. It could even help the demons learn things to make their punishments more effective. For example, we would most certainly ask the question, what punishment do you fear the most?

Well, wait a sec. The Hellions are a savvy lot, and they are highly likely to answer with things like "mud baths" and "fruit cups" to try and get the demons confused. And if you asked things like "What did you do to get sentenced to eternal damnation?" you'd never get an honest answer.

OK, OK. Dumb idea.

CHAPTER 27

HAPPY HOUR

After LPOD heard about the challenges to Black Friday, things got hotter. I was hanging around my cell when I realized that the scorch was at an all-time high. I couldn't even lie on my wrought-iron bed. The metal felt like it was searing my soul. So I sat in a corner and thought about what a crazy path I had taken.

My life in Hell was about to change for the worse, one way or another. I was just sure of it. This wasn't me just being negative. I used to be that guy. Always expecting the worst. Thinking that the half-empty glass would leak or something.

I thought of that guy topside who had come up with that pretty interesting idea to counter Black Friday craziness. Can you believe how awful it would be to be assigned a store like that for *Jingle Hell*? Say that Hell never got the news that some retailer was shutting down on Black Friday, and you just bubbled up from the plumbing and the place was dark as the crypt. You frantically look around looking for targets, and there are none. You float around and there's no one there.

Although, I had to admit—what a really solid idea if you really cared about people. (And then I thought, man, did I just think that?) Why not keep people out of the craziness and encourage them do something good for their bodies, if not their souls. And although I was never a businessperson, I had an inkling that that guy Stew might be super good for his business. Just not mine, unfortunately.

Sometime later, I was gathered up by some security demons who marched me out of my cell to a cavern that seemed three weeks away. As I entered the gloomy spot, I was surprised to see Team Brimstone standing around and talking like they were at a cocktail party. They all looked my way and waved, smiling. It was surreal. I felt like I was meeting friends at a happy hour.

I walked over, grinning like a fool myself. Pirate gave me a slap on the back, Genghis a fist bump (now where did he learn that?), and Sticks shook my hand and said, "Great to see you, Laverne" with that winning, I've-got-a-deal-for-you smile of his that also charmed the pants off of everyone—including me. I nodded to Floris, who was as always aloof. And yes, Simone gave me a smile and a wink, and then she leaned in and planted a long, very hot kiss on my cheek. If I hadn't been in Hell I would have said I was in Heaven.

It was funny, but topside I had never really had any kind of really serious relationship. I was too self-absorbed, too selfish and too much into my music to be good for anyone—including myself, I guess. Who knew I would have to go to Hell to get a girlfriend?

CHAPTER 28

DECLINED

"Asmodeus—that three-headed demon—was here not long ago," said Simone. "It was incredible! He said Satan is really twisted up about something or other that is going on with Black Friday retail this year. Then Asmodeus said that he wanted us to be sure and strategize for the coming competition. He was really nervous looking, too. His sheep head kept bleating that it was his turn to talk, but the bull head was bellowing out orders, and let's just say that the guy spitting fire apparently had a lot of phlegm to clear today."

I laughed and said, "I can tell you what's behind all of that." I recounted to them what LPOD had said to Eligos. Genghis clearly didn't understand much. He just smiled and tilted his head. Pirate somehow seemed to get the gist. The rest got it loud and clear.

"Wow," said Sticks, scratching his chin. "Can't see it exactly becoming a huge trend due to the money involved with Black Friday, but I can see some other businesses jumping on the bandwagon."

ASMODEUS

A full 72 legions of demons report to Asmodeus. He is primarily known for his appearance in the biblical story of Tobit, in which he was attracted to Sarah, Raguel's daughter, and would not let any husband possess her. He was so obsessed that he murdered each of her seven successive husbands on their wedding nights. He is also a part of some Talmudic legends such as the story of the construction of the Temple of Solomon, in which Asmodeus was tricked by Solomon to lend a hand. He is known as the demon of lust and oversees all gambling houses in the court of Hell.

In the Dictionnaire Infernal, Asmodeus sits atop a lion with dragon's wings and neck and has three heads – a man's that is breathing fire, as well as those of both a sheep and a bull. He has a human torso, rooster legs, and a serpent's tail.

Asmodeus was cited by the nuns of Loudun (France) during the Loudun Possessions in 1634, in which a convent of Ursuline sisters said they had been visited and possessed by demons.

Aliases

⁑⁑⁑⁑⁑⁑⁑⁑⁑⁑⁑⁑⁑⁑⁑⁑⁑⁑⁑⁑⁑⁑⁑⁑⁑

Asmodaios	*Asmodeo*
Asmodai	*Asmodeu*
Asmodeios	*Asmodeius*
Ashmedai	*Asmodi*
Ashmadia	*Chammaday*
Ashmodai	*Chasmodai*
Asmoday	*Sidonay*
Asmodee	*Sydonai*

Abilities

⁑⁑⁑⁑⁑⁑⁑⁑⁑⁑⁑⁑⁑⁑⁑⁑⁑⁑⁑⁑⁑⁑⁑⁑⁑

Asmodeus can:

‡

Manipulate people's sexual desires

‡

Fill human hearts with anger

‡

*Incite humans (particularly men)
to revenge*

‡

Turn people to gambling

‡

*Lead married persons to cheat
on their spouses*

‡

*Confound listeners when speaking
out of multiple mouths*

‡

Sing acapella versions of all Glee
and Pitch Perfect *songs*

⁑⁑⁑⁑⁑⁑⁑⁑⁑⁑⁑⁑⁑⁑⁑⁑⁑⁑⁑⁑⁑⁑⁑⁑⁑

"Yeah, but what's the big deal?" asked Simone. "It can't be that big of a threat, can it?"

"Well, LPOD wants to make this a blockbuster year just to be sure to counter it," I said. "But if I were him, I would actually take a year off. The more chaos we create on Black Friday, the more backlash it's likely to create."

"You're probably right," said Simone. "But we do want to win, right?" We all smiled and got down to strategizing. I sidled next to Simone, and she glanced my way, knowingly.

We had learned quite a bit during our last two years, of course. That and a little creativity gave birth to such strategies as:

· The "Queue" Factor—People in lines behave like swine
· The Family Freak-out—Families shopping together are on a short tether
· The Blue-light Lift—Fighting for steals exposes Achilles heels
· Avoid Smilers—Those who grin are less likely to sin
· Negativity Proclivity—we *love* whiners!

At one point while the others were trying to get an idea together that had something to do with getting checkout people to ask for two forms of IDs with every transaction, Simone turned to me and whispered: "Don't say anything to the others, but although I'm as competitive as the next person, and this has been a lot of fun, I'm beginning to think I've had enough of helping to send people down here. But I really want to see you, Laverne. That's what I would miss most if this all goes away."

I looked at her with amazement. Then I said, "Wow. I've been having some similar thoughts, to be honest. I think it's been just being around you—and the music—that have gotten me to rethink some things lately. I just don't like the idea of sending people down here either."

We were both silent for a bit. Then I asked her, "What do you think we should do?"

"I don't know, Laverne," she said. Then she brightened and said in a loud voice, "How about getting the checkout folks to

randomly tell people that their credit cards were declined. Now *THAT* should work, don't you think?"

That strategy session really was truly a blast. To overcome the language gap with Genghis and, to a lesser extent, Pirate, we drew crude pictures in the cavern dirt and had some real fun doing charades. I taught them *"Jingle Hell,"* and we sang it over and over. At one point Pirate danced some sort of jig to it, singing in his heavy French accent.

When Simone first heard it, she shook her head in wonder and said, "You've got real talent, Laverne. That's ridiculously awesome."

She even liked my music. Deep longing sigh.

CHAPTER 29

SIGILS

It was right about then that I had another one of my really weird dreams. I was going onstage at some sort of county fair. I could smell the beer and hamburgers, the cotton candy, the buttery ears of corn, the fried Oreos. Yuck. It was night, and the lights of the Tilt-a-Whirl, the Ferris Wheel, and the Scrambler were crazily blinking off to the left. To the right were the games. The pump-action guns that shot corks. The basketball game with the ridiculously small rims. The ring toss game where you won goldfish in bulging plastic bags. For some reason all of the fish were red, though. It was dusty and hot, but the beer was icy cold, served in sweating red plastic cups. I knew that because I was holding one. It was so real.

My bandmates and I were setting up. No roadies for us at that point. It was the old days. I had just plugged in my Tempest, tuned it, and put it in its stand. I was about to grab the mic stand when I noticed that the sigils on the guitar were glowing.

"What the ...," I said, staring at the guitar. They started glowing even brighter. I couldn't believe my eyes. Wow, if I could perform with them glowing like that it would be incredible, I thought to myself. Then they were pulsing red. It looked like they were going to burn right through the alder wood body, but I didn't see any smoke.

"LAVERNE!"

I was horrified. No one in my band even knew my name was Laverne. Was this an old childhood friend or something?

As I looked for the owner of that voice, I noticed that its sound had sort of sliced through the carny noise, and the world appeared to spin down and go dead and silent. The white hanging lights in the tent still glowed and swayed in the breeze, but it was as if the entire fair and all the other people in it had hit pause. It was LPOD, and it was just him and me in that moment of the universe.

"Laverne, it is time," LPOD said.

"Time for what, LPOD?'

"It's time for a new start, Laverne."

"OK ...," I said.

"Some of my demons are getting very cross with you, and it is difficult to hold them in check," LPOD said. "So I don't think I *will ANY LONGER*. "

I heard a puffing sound to my side. I glanced down and saw a small demon next to my guitar. He was pumping a large bellows furiously, now fanning what had become leaping flames that poured out of the sigils on my guitar. The neck was beginning to blacken, and the strings were even glowing. I yelled, "Hey, stop that you little ..." and was headed over there to brain him when the stage opened up below me and I fell into the abyss. As I dropped, thousands of demon eyes looked up at me, and then I heard thunderous, terrifying laughter.

I came to in a hot sweat. (There is no cold version in Hell, of course.)

CHAPTER 30

EXTRACTION

I had the general sense that Black Friday was getting near, but I of course had been relieved of my iPhone and "Guitar Heroes of Rock" wall calendar so I really had no clear idea. I was on the Plain of Sorrows receiving more of my just desserts. This time it was really a savory one—one of the worst tortures that Hell has on offer.

My anxiety level was already off the charts, and I was having to deal with this. Unbelievable. It was incredibly punishing, draining and demoralizing. I was leaning back in that awful chair, thinking that it was finally over and I could go back to my cell, when Eurynome said in that incredibly whiny voice of his, "Well, I found another cracked tooth, Laverne. It will have to be extracted."

Eurynome has the most terrifying teeth of any demon in Hell. A real serrated smile on that one. I swear he files them. And I suppose it is no surprise that he is absolutely passionate about dental care.

EURYNOME

Eurynome is a rather cringey looking demon who wears fox skins to hide the sores that have erupted over his body.

Pausanias, a Greek traveler and geographer from the second century A.D., wrote of a painting of Hades by Polygnotos at Delphi, Phocis. His Delphinian guides pointed out Eurynome, a netherworld daemon (spirit) who eats the flesh of rotting corpses. (Now you know why he has skin trouble.) Describing the painting, Pausanias said Eurynome was "a colour between blue and black, like that of meat flies; he is showing his teeth and is seated, and under him is spread a vulture's skin."

Other than the reference by Pausanias and de Plancy's Dictionnaire Infernal entry, mentions of Eurynome are scarce until he became a bit of a pop culture darling in more recent years. He took a star turn in Umberto Ecco's book *Foucault's Pendulum*, although Ecco's ignominious typo presented him as "Eurynomius." In the 1977 film Dead of Night, he was invoked by a grieving mother who turns to a rite in the Lesser Key of Solomon‡ in the hope of reviving her drowned son.

ALIASES

****

Eurynomos
Eurynomius
(if you count Ecco's goof)

ABILITIES

****

Eurynome can:

‡

Control the movement of air

‡

Turn tides

‡

Eat just about anything

‡

Dry out wet mobile phones

‡

Foul water sources

‡

Test the limits of the most formidable personal hygiene products

****

---

‡ The *Lesser Key of Solomon* is an anonymously penned spell book, or grimoire, that first appeared in the mid-1600s. It is partially based on material that was hundreds of years old at the time of the book's first printing, and it includes information on 72 demons.

"But you've already taken four today, and that tooth isn't hurting at all. Couldn't we just wait and see on that one?" I pleaded.

"Now Laverne, this could really cause you some serious complications. You don't want that, do you?" Eurynome chided. With that he picked up a grimy set of pliers and reached in ....

I groaned.

As he leaned over me and peered into my mouth, putting his other incredibly hairy elbow on my chest to gain leverage, he said, "Are you and Team Brimstone ready for action this year?"

"Ah hah," I muttered. "Weddy as wey e-er ahhh."

"Well, this is going to be an interesting one this year, Laverne, or—is it Dirk nowadays? Oh well. Laverne. I'm not one to gossip, but this is going to be a mighty interesting year!"

I felt a ripping in my jaw and groaned loudly.

"Oh shoot, Laverne. I only got part of it. He gleefully showed me what was clenched in the nasty jaws of the pliers. "I'm going to have to have another go, I'm afraid. Be done in a heartbeat. Hah! Not that you have one!"

I shuddered.

"It appears that several weeks ago, several major retailers began to get on the 'be with your family, be active, be out-of-doors'—frankly—'be anywhere but in the store' bandwagon," Eurynome said. "LPOD is apparently beside himself. He's sending all sorts of demons up there to try to counter this thing."

I heard a flapping noise and realized something or somebody was landing over to my left.

"Eligos! How goes it?" said Eurynome. "Give me just a minute. I'm extracting a nasty cracked tooth fragment out of old Laverne here."

"Certainly, Eurynome. Take your time," said Eligos.

Eligos walked into my line of sight. He looked grave.

I felt another ripping sensation.

"Ah, got it!" said Eurynome.

"Hurrah," Eligos deadpanned as he turned his head to the side and rolled his eyes. His steed even snorted dismissively.

"There we are," said Eurynome. He dropped the tooth fragment into the tray to his right, turned off the examination lamp and said. "Swish and spit, Laverne. And just wait for me here. I will be right back." I sincerely hoped not.

He walked off to my right, gesturing Eligos to come with him. The two of them strolled a bit, conferring quietly. I tried my best to eavesdrop.

Eligos: "No luck ... very difficult ... LPOD is REALLY ..."

Eurynome: "Oh boy ... [shocked sounding exclamation] ... what can I ... "

Eligos: "Need you ... imperative that ... not an option ..."

Eurynome: "Of course ... happy to ... sounds extremely ... strategy ..."

They then strolled a bit further and I could no longer make out any words. I was fascinated, though. It sounded like Eligos' efforts might be failing. Maybe the anti-Black-Friday forces were gathering strength? I was torn, though. I was part of the machine, for Pete's sake. Part of the *Jingle Hell* program. A friggin star of the program. But at the same time, I couldn't help but feel like cheering on those who were trying their best to refocus things a bit topside. I remembered my conversation with Simone.

Eurynome and Eligos walked back muttering to one another. Then I very distinctly heard Eligos say something about "The 27 Project." I gulped, wondering if I myself had been a victim of that one.

Eligos mounted that malnourished looking skeletal horse of his and they flew off with a strong flap or two. The flapping must have wafted back to me the odor of the beast, which smelled like the summertime dumpster behind the Burger Worx where I had gotten my first job.

Eurynome leaned over me grinning like a maniac with those gigantic teeth of his and said, "You really should take better care of those teeth, Dirk! See you next time!" I almost passed out in relief and left without a wisecrack. I was pretty sure that he might have me back in the chair in an instant if I made any smart (or not-so-smart) comments.

Two security demons approached with the next patient. Now you would never guess this would happen in a place with zillions of residents, but it was Simone. I saw her before she saw me. I was undoubtedly not looking my suave, confident best at that moment, so my first thought was I really didn't want her to see me. But then I saw her look of fear and loathing as she was being led to the chair. It broke my heart, and the pain from that totally trumped the agony from my aching mouth.

Then she saw me, and I could tell she immediately refocused on *my* pain. Her look of concern was one of the sweetest things I had seen since I passed through the grimy Gates of Hell. It was like sunshine breaking through a bank of slate-gray rain clouds. We were too far away to speak to one another, but she winked at me. I did my best to give her my crooked, LPOD-may-care smile (which is really, really not easy when you've just lost five teeth), and then I was led out by the security demons.

I heard Simone say unusually loudly, "I *love* that smile!" Eurynome said, "Well thank you, my dear!"

My heart leapt for a moment. Then, as the security demon roughly pushed me forward, I looked over my shoulder and saw her sitting down in that chair.

CHAPTER 31

PEP RALLY

It was the strangest thing—sort of like a pep rally in Hell. Apparently, the anti-Black Friday forces had driven LPOD to some very unusual lengths. Tens of thousands of demons and GDHD agents filled the throne cavern. The B.O. in there was off-the-charts ridiculous.

"Tomorrow you glorious *Jingle Hell* teams go once more unto the breach," shouted LPOD. "You not only bring us top-quality entertainment, but, more importantly, you help to further the cause of evil and deliver the souls of the damned. To be honest, it makes me rather misty thinking about the success of this show over the years." He paused as if he really needed to gather himself. "We are all truly a part of something special. Something that evokes the very culture we cultivate here in Hell. A legacy of licentiousness. A heritage of hate. A tradition of the incomprehensibly indecent. It's truly what makes us family down here." He smiled benevolently.

The crowd applauded enthusiastically, many snorting with gusto and stomping their feet until the cavern vibrated. Pazuzu

and Melchom, both standing to LPOD's right, were humbly
looking down at their feet. Then Melchom looked at Pazuzu,
scowled, and moved away from him. Pazuzu looked around
guiltily. I realized he must have broken his evil wind again.

"As one of our most accomplished—and shortest, heh
heh—residents down here once said, 'Impossible is a word to
be found only in the dictionary of fools.'" LPOD nodded to
some very short, greasy-haired guy in an old blue and white
military uniform and funny hat with his left hand stuck
into his jacket as if he had acid reflux. "So, despite the new
challenges we face topside, we still expect great things from
our *Jingle Hell* teams this season." LPOD nodded to Pazuzu,
who stepped forward.

"Team Brihhhhhhmstone, with an unprehhhhhhhcedented
two years of wihhhhhhns unhhhhhhder its belt, will defend
ihhhhhhhhts tighhhhhhhtle against Team Suhhhhhhlphur, Team
Hehhhhhhhllfire and Team Politishhhhhhian. As ahhhhhhhlways,
may the behhhhhst team win! Yehhhhhhhhhs!" He then belched
loudly.

Again, spirited applause, snorts and stomping. I happened
to glance at LPOD at that very moment. I could have sworn he
was looking right at me and grinning. And then—this made
me shudder—he *actually* appeared to wink at me. I didn't know
what to do, so I just nodded in what I hoped was a respectful
manner, and then kept my eyes downcast.

Melchom walked forward. "Today we have a very
special guest with us. A Hellion who as a famous artist
both topside and here in Hell has done so much to help us

add to the Underworld's rich tapestry of horrors, tortures, and instruments of pain and suffering. Just a few of his contributions include what I daresay are some of our all-time favorites—those hideously wonderful snails with human legs, fish with human arms that eat souls whole, lizard-dogs that make Rottweilers look like Care Bears, and spider-legged peacocks—all beautiful, but *extremely* dangerous."

I had once been chased by one of those. They were very, very fast. And those snails tended to have female human legs, so I had dubbed them the Escar-Go-Go-Girls.

Melchom continued, "He's also the soul who thought up such delightful damnations as sitting on giant knife blades, being immersed in barrels with piranhas and leeches, being impaled upon harp strings and other such deliciously playful things. Allow me to introduce you toooooo ... Hieronymus Bosch!"

The applause was polite. No snorts and stamping, but polite. A strange looking man walked up to the dais in what looked like medieval dress, complete with a strange floppy cloth hat that looked a little bit like a 1940s football helmet.

The man waved to the crowd and babbled something in a language that sounded like the Dutch Floris spoke. It was quick, and then he left. The security demon to my left said to another demon: "I've got some of his latest 'Scenes from Hell' stuff in my cavern. One of them is a black light poster and I could stare at it for hours. It's truly *inspirational*!" He certainly looked inspired.

Then the cavern went completely and totally dark. I looked around and saw only the glowing eyes of the demons.

LPODs voice boomed out: "Just as none of us ever fear the dark, we also do not fear the forces that have conspired to damage Black Friday. I ask you all to reaffirm with me your allegiance to the Black, to our home—Hell! Say it with me now. HELL! HELL! HELL!" The demons shouted the word. At first it was just with gusto. Then it became maniacal. Other contestants were doing the same. My team was as well, except for Simone. She turned and looked at me, met my gaze, and held it.

Then what looked to be four enormous spotlights flicked on. They pointed straight up into the depths of the cavern. It was then that I saw for the first time how tall the cavern was. I literally could not see a roof, despite the piercing beams of light.

The chanting got even louder. "Now, contestants, go back to your cells, steel your resolve and prepare yourself for the best *Jingle Hell* competition EVER!" He joined in the crazed chanting himself as we were led out of the cavern. On the way out, all of the teams were handed Shamrock Shakes. I shit you not.

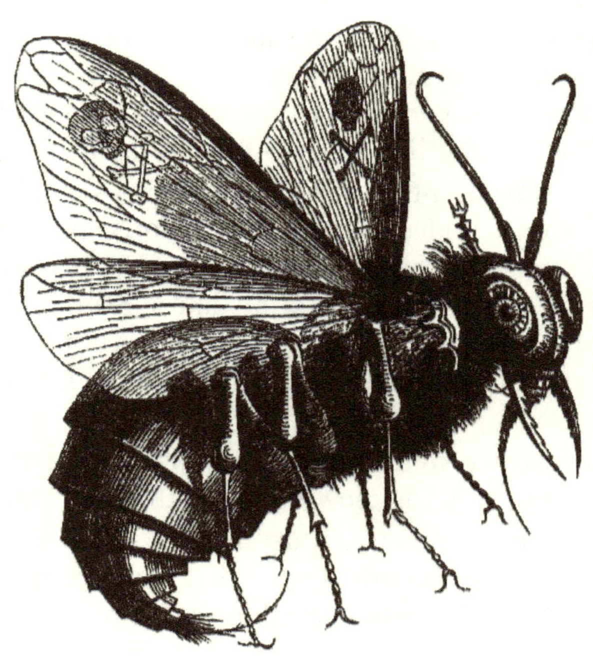

CHAPTER 32

BACK

Well, here I am, back to where I started this story. I could still hear that *incredibly* annoying flying, dismembered head shrieking down the cell block hall, "Another Day in Paradise, Hellions!" I looked around the cell. My guitar and amp were still there in the corner. At least that was going my way. For now. I thought about playing a little, and then I just clasped my hands behind my head and settled back onto my rack.

My third season of *Jingle Hell* was just around the corner. Time really had flown. I *had* relearned some pretty amazing things about the power of music during the last several years. Even more miraculous given my environs, I had learned about love. On that score, it was pretty much the first time for me.

If one were looking for cosmic can't-misses, those two would be high on the list. But here I was, preparing to once again pop up through some nasty retail restroom plumbing and help condemn hundreds of people to the same kind of eternal suffering and torture top-40s that I had to look forward to. *"I'm on a Segway to Hell,"* as one of my AC/DC knockoffs had put it. But now I was having a serious existential crisis. I just wasn't sure how I felt about sullying souls anymore.

I knew from the previous three years that there would not be any torture today. I suppose they wanted us on our A-game as we softened the beaches for the GDHD operatives. But the heat was up. No break there from the management. The tick, tick of the radiators against the wall kept time with my despair. What I would give now for some sort of ice cream novelty.

Actually, what I really wanted was to just sit around with Simone. As I mentioned before, you don't really get "hot" in Hell. Pleasure of any sort is, of course, frowned upon. But I remembered how my Grandpa and Grandma on my mom's side always held hands when they took walks, or even if they were sitting and watching TV. I supposed how I felt about Simone might be pretty similar.

I reconsidered my decision not to play guitar. I stood up, walked over, uncased the Strat and slung it over my shoulder. I wondered to myself if this was going to be my last opportunity to play. Ever. I decided I wasn't going to stop until they came for me.

'Tis the season to not take anything for granted, I thought to myself.

CHAPTER 33

THREE PEAT

On the march to the plane, the tension was unlike anything we had experienced so far. On one side, we had the benefit of being two-time champions. But I could tell that did not translate to overconfidence for any one of us. Even good-natured Pirate seemed a little reserved, like he was about to be boarded by two English warships. We of course knew the chances of three-peating were awfully low. We had sized up the other teams at the rally, and they looked confident and pretty solid, although who knew what they would be like in the field. This time we had also not been told where we were going, so that added to our stress.

Of course, I also knew the stakes were higher than ever before in terms of what I had to look forward to if I lost. A vision of Lamashtu skittering across my cell ceiling popped into my mind. I shuddered.

The security demons seemed a bit more tense than usual this time. They had sternly warned us not to talk. Of course, we still snuck some snippets of conversation in, and it was even easier once we got to the plane. As soon as the security demons were busy at the control panel, I managed to have some words with Simone. She was the closest to the cockpit and I was next to her, so we were whispering carefully. At the same time, Sticks and Pirate were grinning like madmen. I could see they were playing rock, paper, scissors.

"What are you thinking?" I asked her. "You still feeling like this is all wrong?"

"Sure," she answered. "But I suppose we have to go with the 'When in Rome' approach." She sighed deeply. "Oh, I wish I wouldn't have said that. Wouldn't it be wonderful to be in Rome? I would take you to this wonderful old-school restaurant where they make the most amazing trofie."

"What's that?" I asked.

"I like to call it 'prayer pasta' because you make it by putting a little pasta in the center of one of your palms, then put the other hand right over it like you are praying and then move your hands back and forth to create the shape—thicker in the middle and thinner on the sides."

I thought about how wonderful it would be to have a dinner of trofie and a nice bottle of wine with Simone. And in Rome. I had never been there. Did the residents of heaven get to visit such places—or at least heavenly equivalents? Then I thought how truly odd it was for Simone to be referencing anything related to praying.

One of the security demons—a guy with a particularly sinister looking beaked nose—looked over his shoulder at us. I stared straight ahead and he went back to his glowing instruments.

I turned to Simone. "Well, we might as well win one more time, don't you think?" I whispered.

"Yup," she answered. She winked at me and smiled. Then we were quiet.

The light above me and to the right went red. The other security demon said, "GET READY! GET UP!" He pointed to Pirate, who was closest to the hole. "GET IN POSITION." I heard the gurgling noise again. About ten seconds passed.

"GO GO GO GO GO!" the demon yelled. Pirate flew up the pipe. As did Floris, then Genghis, then Sticks, all of us moving forward steadily. I was next. The plane lurched hard, then I heard Simone behind me, right at my ear, cooing in a sexy voice, "Hey. You have a *really* nice –" w h o o o o s h . I was gone.

I eventually heard another gurgling noise and this time, as I entered the light, I realized I had emerged through a urinal. Unbelievable.

I passed out of the john as quickly as I could and entered a scene that completely disoriented me. For a good minute or two, I just stared at my surroundings. Something was wrong, but I couldn't draw a bead on exactly what at first. It slowly dawned on me.

LPOD had sent us to a Plush Productions store. Stuffed animals filled shelves everywhere. Teddy bears, giraffes, dinosaurs, raccoons, foxes, moose, whales, hippos, elephants, even stuffed tacos and pancake stacks with butter pat noses. Banners throughout the store proclaimed, "Cuddly Friend Friday—Everything 10% Off!!!!!"

This was a Black Friday train wreck. If I had had a physical presence, I would have kicked the stuffing out of hundred or so teddy bears. Not only was the store probably the worst one we could have been sent to in terms of size—other than a 7-Eleven or something—but the storewide sale meant that no one was going to be worried about getting THE deal, the last item on sale, the exclusive purchase that everyone coveted. NO clawing, no yelling, no grasping, no hating one's fellow shopper. We were screwed.

I glanced at the team. They were all gawking and clearly as dazed and confused as I was. Except for Floris, that is. He looked like he had just won the lottery. Geez.

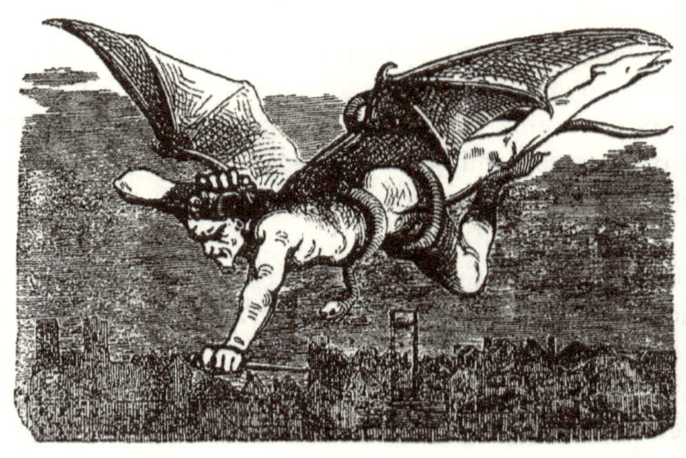

CHAPTER 34

PLANS

Then I noticed something. At the far end of the fairly small store—this was no Shopmart, to be sure—I saw that a small stage was set up. Some guy in his late forties or early fifties was tuning an acoustic guitar in front of a banner that said "Billy's Boulevard." The banner showed this cartoony residential street with happy looking birds sitting in big leafy trees and creepy looking kids playing in front yards.

I remembered this middle-aged hipster dude. He had been in a one-hit-wonder band, and then went into recording and performing kids' music. Although I had heard he was making pretty good money doing it, the thought of becoming like this guy was my worst nightmare when I was among the living. No matter what happened with my music career, I NEVER wanted to be a kids' artist. Listen, no offense intended. It just wasn't for me. Nothing against kids, you know.

Could this be a further kick in the teeth delivered by LPOD, I thought to myself? Oh yeah, sure ... now I began to see it. A message about what was in store for me when I got back. It was all downhill from here.

I started to get even angrier.

Then the smiling, super friendly looking employees turned the locks and the store was open for business. (Of course, Plush Productions let you in a little early.) Each was wearing a teddy bear shaped name badge on a bright yellow golf shirt, and khakis. They courteously greeted all the incoming customers as if their lives depended on it.

And the shoppers filed in politely. They were ridiculously happy looking as well. Many of them chatted amicably with their fellow shoppers. No pushing, no anger, no good-old-fashioned aggression. It was like a convention of preschool teachers. Almost immediately, plush toys were being piled into shopping baskets like cordwood.

Simone glided over to me, raising her eyebrows and shaking her head tightly. She was REALLY angry. I had never seen her that mad before.

"This is pointless, stupid, and a total waste of our time. LPOD TOTALLY has it out for us! This is SO UNFAIR!!!!"

"Yeah, I know," I answered in a quiet whisper, tapping my ear. "I gather that LPOD and his demons have had enough of us winning all the time." I looked around, smiling innocently, knowing full well that we were on-air. "We're like the Lebron James' of the Underworld. The Tom Bradys of Hades."

Simone gathered herself and forced a smile. She made an odd growling noise. I could tell how she had been successful in the tech sector. She was ultra-competitive, yet at the same time she could control herself. I'm sure there were a lot of meetings in her career where she couldn't let the other side of the table know how she was feeling. I couldn't help but thinking, though, that she had certainly never gone up against a competitor like LPOD.

Then I had an idea. I read once that the essence of creativity involved putting things together in new combinations. I was going to do just that.

I leaned over to whisper in her ear. "Simone, I've got an idea. I'm only suggesting it because we're already condemned to Hell and, well, things couldn't get much worse than that. Having said that, you would still have to be open to the possibility that they might."

She looked at me, raised her eyebrows and then leaned in conspiratorially.

"Pray tell, Laverne."

It was a simple plot. But at the same time, it fit that old saw: Make no small plans. It was definitely big, although we had no idea just *how* big at the time.

CHAPTER 35

BULLET

I can only imagine that the show producers killed our feed at a certain point. But I was quite sure that it wasn't early enough. Oh, yes, I was quite sure of that. The security demons at the plane hustled us back to our cells very, very roughly. It was almost as if they didn't want to be near us any longer than they had to be. No "after party" this time. No basking in the red glow of the Evilometer.

At the same time, I was also pretty confident that they did not understand what Simone was up to while I was working on Billy. I really hoped I was right on that count.

It certainly was hotter in my cell after that. And as you have probably guessed, the guitar and amp were gone. Other than that, though, things became unsettlingly quiet.

Whatever happened next, I was also sure that I had made a colossal mistake getting Simone involved. I felt gut-wrenchingly, over-the-top terrible about it. For weeks I stared into black corners and worried about her. But I was sure that the larger plan wouldn't have ever worked without her.

ALASTER

Zoroaster, the Persian religious teacher who probably lived in the sixth or seventh century B.C., called Alaster "the executioner." He takes the appearance of a powerful, white-eyed, human-bodied creature with an animal head and face that reminds one of a wolf. In the hierarchy of demons he is known as the Nemesis, the agent of divine punishment for wrongdoing or presumption.

If he carried a business card, it would present two titles: Grand Torturer of Hell and Chief Executor of Decrees. Regarding the latter, he often serves as LPOD's right hand. All other demons apprentice in torture under him, although none have ever reached his level of excruciating skill at the art.

He can travel between Hell and Earth instantaneously, a skill LPOD does not allow many demons to possess for relatively obvious security reasons. (And as you can imagine, LPOD has some very deep-seated trust issues.) This visitation ability allows Alaster the opportunity to keep in touch with pop culture and therefore devise tortures that masterfully "fit the times" of those who find themselves eternally damned. He is known for his unmatched cruelty and sadism. Even other demons fear him.

The ancients called evil spirits "alastores." Plutarch wrote that the Roman politician Cicero hated Emperor Augustus so much that he once considered committing suicide outside Augustus' foyer in the hopes that he would become Augustus' resident alaster.

ALIASES

****

Alastair
Azazel

ABILITIES

****

Alaster can:
‡
*Quickly uncover humans'
weaknesses*
‡
Spread pestilence
‡
*Lead men to commit unspeakable
crimes*
‡
*Name any pop song in five
or fewer notes*
‡
*Recite the start-to-finish dialogue
of any Disney Princess movie*

****

Memories are long in Hell, however. I knew that I was going to have to live with the fallout for eternity, of course, but the realization that I might have made her existence innumerably worse was almost unbearable.

I was obsessing over all of this when my cell door crashed open and the demon Alaster strode in, *People* magazine under his arm. My heart sunk, but I tried to put on a brave face.

"Alaster, how incredibly thoughtful. I haven't had a chance to read *People* in ages," I said.

A slight grin crossed his face. "Don't be cheeky, Laverne," he said. His right eyebrow arched upward. "You're liable to make me try some new techniques on you for a decade or two."

My heart now hit sub-basement level 3 and kept plummeting. Alaster is to torture what fluorescent green pickle relish is to Chicago hot dogs.

"In fact, you are quite fortunate, Laverne. Today I am simply here on a fact-finding mission," he said. "If I find you cooperative, your next millennium or two might be a teensy weensy bit less excruciating for you. If I find you uncooperative, I have a regimen that involves both delicious levels of pain and boy band music that we can begin without further ado."

I winced.

"What in the world did you do up there, you silly boy?"

I looked down at my scorched feet. I wasn't exactly sure how to play things with Alaster. Every demon was a little different, of course, and with my obsessing about Simone, I hadn't really gotten around to brainstorming an approach for him. That was dumb—and dangerous.

"Laverne, I have no patience today," said Alaster. "You have somehow created a right fine shitstorm topside. LPOD is not amused. Therefore, neither am I." He shouted toward the door, "Bring in my things."

The door swung open and two security demons walked in. One was carrying a boombox and the other one hefted a large glass jar filled with something black—something that was moving. I cringed and pulled back. They looked like spiders or black bugs of some kind. I was terrified of bugs and spiders. Even down here, with all of the other things to terrify you on a daily basis.

"Now I happen to know that you abhor bugs and spiders, and that boy band music makes you experience intense revulsion and despair," said Alaster. "The two of them together should do the trick! This boombox will play boy band medleys directly into your consciousness, such as it is." He smirked.

"Then, this jar is filled with a very special treat. These rather unassuming inch-long ants are really, really fun! They deliver what many believe is the most agonizing sting in the insect world. I'm sure you are probably not familiar with the Schmidt Pain Index, but I of course am. That widely respected, four-level pain scale for the stings of wasps, bees, ants, and sawflies—now *there* is a name that gives a demon some ideas—gives these little guys a four and describes their sting as 'pure, intense, brilliant pain.' *Travel & Leisure* magazine said it is 'like fire-walking over flaming charcoal with a three-inch rusty nail in your heel.' They go on to say that victims who have suffered both being stung by this ant and being shot with a firearm say the pain is similar. I could go on, but I won't because we should just get started, don't you think?"

Alaster reached into the jar and brought out one tiny ant. It crawled around on his palm, and then to the end of Alaster's index finger. It paused there and seemed to be looking at me.

"All the way from the rainforests of Central America, Laverne, please meet the *BULLET ant*!"

He held it out to me. I shrunk back against the wall. I was ready to spill *almost* everything.

i SING

My stomach plunged to sub-basement 33 this time and kept hurtling down. One thing you quickly learn in Hell is that there is no reason to go for style points. I knew I was licked. But there was absolutely no way I was going to give up Simone to this sadistic, pop-culture-nutcase-freakshow.

"You can put that little guy right back in its jar, Alaster," I said. "There's no need for me to make his or her acquaintance today."

Alaster said, "Aw darn," and shook his head forlornly. "You're no fun, Laverne. That was way too easy." Frowning, he unscrewed the jar and flicked the ant inside.

Then he appeared to brighten up a bit, his eyebrows lifting and mouth opening in a playful smile. "But I'm pretty sure you will lie to me, in which case I will have you experience my friends here at some point in the near future! Or maybe you should just get stung one time, just to help our conversation along a bit!" He began to unscrew the jar again excitedly.

"No, no, no, Alaster! Really! I'll tell you everything you want to know!" I was pleading at that point. Thankfully, he put the jar down and said, "Oh, all right then! No fun, no fun, no FUN!"

Then I told him *almost* all of the story. Thankfully, Melchom wasn't there. He was the one I really needed to worry about. Melchom was able to get inside your head and squeeze out secrets just like he was crushing a juicy orange. All the while he would look at you with this slight, knowing smile on his lips.

Listen, for a guy like Billy who made his living playing little-person hits, what I did in that store helped him take a big step up, if you ask me. And although conning the little people to learn their numbers, coercing them to think happily about school, or tricking them to eat veggies were certainly admirable causes, ol' Billy had no idea what he could accomplish with me whispering in his ear. I gave him the song *"Jingle Hell"* that day. He performed it on site, then recorded it. It went platinum. Billy became famous overnight, albeit in a rather unconventional, Bob-Dylan-meets-Adam-Sandler kind of way. At least that's what I later found out.

With those ants eyeing me through the jar, I sang like a bird. I spilled my guts like the Deepwater Horizon. It wasn't pretty. But I absolutely did not mention Simone.

It was funny. When I was soul whispering to Billy, it just felt so easy. Like taking candy from a baby, putty in my hands, a walk in the park, a layup, easy peasy lemon squeezy. But it wasn't just that it was easy. It also felt right. For the first time in an awfully long time, I felt like I was doing something for the good side, rather than just for myself. Of course, I knew it was too late for me in all of the most important ways, but it just felt good. Better than the triple encore I once got at the Winnebago County Fair.

JINGLE HELL

Dashing through the aisles
Clawing for a deal
Making greedy piles
Makes me want to squeal
Bells on registers ring
The Evilometer's bright
Oh what fun it is to serve the King
We're sullying souls tonight

Jingle Hell, Jingle Hell
Jingle all the way
Oh what fun
It is to lead
Black Friday mortals astray. Hey!
Jingle Hell, Jingle Hell
Jingle all the way
Oh what fun
It is to lead
Black Friday mortals astray

A month or two ago
The first decorations were hung
Go with the commercial flow
You'll be kissed by the serpent's
  tongue
The sales tempt souls like gold
Greed and envy drive the day
Through Hell's gates you'll roll
Your ticket is one-way

Jingle Hell, Jingle Hell
Jingle all the way
Oh what fun
It is to lead
Black Friday mortals astray. Hey!
Jingle Hell, Jingle Hell
Jingle all the way
Oh what fun
It is to lead
Black Friday mortals astray

Now the souls are growing black
As shoppers spend more green
Keep it up, Jill and Jack
Turn on to the demon scene
Our agents are ready to pounce
They're chomping at the bit
And tallying the counts
Of souls that are not worth a spit

Jingle Hell, Jingle Hell
Jingle all the way
Oh what fun
It is to lead
Black Friday mortals astray. Hey!
Jingle Hell, Jingle Hell
Jingle all the way
Oh what fun
It is to lead
Black Friday mortals astray

CHAPTER 37

CANCELLED

Although I had dodged a bullet (heh) with those ants, I did spend what seemed to be the next year or so in the Hills of Wraith. It is not a nice place. The constant shrieking of the wraiths alone was enough to have you wish for a nice bed of nails, or a fire walk. They didn't have those types of pedestrian tortures, there, though. No, not at all. Those punishments are like playing mini golf compared to the Pebble-Beach-level tortures Alaster has lying around in what the residents call "The Hills." I should also note that the sulfur funk there is over-the-top nasty.

The landscape is dotted with menacing plinths with hammered iron rings attached to them so as to provide handy torture tie downs. I was hanging off of one of those, awaiting the arrival of some of Alaster's imps who were wheeling up a smoking, fiery torture device we Hellions called "Hot Wings," when one of them looked up at me and cautiously said, "You know, I saw you after that very first time you and Team Brimstone were on the show."

I raised my eyebrows just a bit in mock interest. It's best to always play along with these guys. His partner scowled at him and shook his head while stoking the fire in Hot Wings, but the first imp continued.

"I have to tell you, I know you had some other amazing shows, but that was my favorite episode ever!" the imp gushed. "I remember almost splitting a gut when those two old hags took down that customer service slob toward the end of the program!"

My head hanging, I smiled weakly and nodded again.

"Did you hear that *Jingle Hell* got cancelled?" the imp asked, his grey-shot eyes looking sad.

I lifted my head and stared at him, dumbfounded. "What's that you say?" I asked.

"Yeah, LPOD just made an announcement. He said something about how *Jingle Hell* had 'jumped the shark' or something like that. I'm not sure what that means, but it does sound fun, doesn't it?" He grinned stupidly.

"Wow, you're kidding me," I said, stunned.

The imp cocked an eye and continued in a whisper, leaning in close to me. And oh my, that little fanged mouth of his definitely needed an Altoid.

"I also heard that song you cut and put in that guy's head got really, really big and started some sort of movement up there that is making Black Friday very, very unpopular. LPOD hasn't talked about it officially, but I heard Alaster saying that some do-gooder also passed something called the 666 law, which makes all those idiot shoppers across the country have to pay an extra 6 percent tax if they shop anytime from 6:00 p.m. on Thanksgiving to 6:00 the next morning. Alaster says it looks like we won't even have stores to send teams to this year."

"That's just ... uh, uh, uh unbelievable," I stuttered, shaking my head and looking off into the distance. Simone must have done an incredible job getting all of those other shoppers to promote the song on social media. I know a bunch of them put it up on YouTube. Thankfully, I don't think LPOD and his demons really understand social media, so I don't think

they are ever going to pick up on what Simone was able to
accomplish. At least I desperately hoped that was the case.

The next thing I knew, the imp had turned away quickly
and averted his eyes, almost as if he and I had never been
talking. Then I realized why. I heard LPOD's voice booming
behind me, "Ah, there he is—over there!" He came into my line
of vision, and I realized he was with Pazuzu and Melchom.
My heart sank. These guys showing up was in no way good,
but with Melchom there, I was absolutely terrified for Simone's
sake. I knew I was already doomed, but if he wanted to break
into my mind he most certainly could. There was no way I
would be able to shield Simone's involvement from him. I
began to panic, then I realized that was the worst thing to
do. So I bit my lip and tried to chill, despite the Hot Wings
machine only feet away. It didn't work.

HOT WINGS

"Don't look so worried, Laverne! I'm going to give you another chance to win a bunch of cold showers and ice cream novelties!" He laughed maniacally. It was the weirdest fake laugh I have ever heard. He was clearly trying to spin events positively. Pazuzu and Melchom both grinned and chuckled. It was bizarre.

"I've got a fantastic new program in development, Laverne, and I need another theme song," LPOD said. "To be honest, I've already turned to some other Hellions for this assignment, but it's clear to me that they just don't get it. I need your special brand of modest musical talent and campy humor. These other guys are just hacks. Which is why I have some demons hacking into them right now!"

LPOD broke out into a hearty laugh again, and this time it wasn't fake at all. Pazuzu and Melchom bellowed out guffaws this time—until Pazuzu farted loudly. LPOD stopped laughing immediately, and the two other demons followed his lead, looking uncomfortable. LPOD turned his head away in disgust and rolled his eyes.

"I would be happy to help, LPOD. Absolutely. Of course. It would be an honor." I tried to sound like a can-do go-getter who is ready to get back to work. It came out more like I had just gotten caught peeking into the neighbor girl's window at night.

Then I asked in a rather meek voice, "So I can get my guitar and amp back? I can't write without those, you know." I glanced at Melchom, but he didn't look suspicious at all. I filled my mind with non-secret thoughts, trying to hide the unspeakable like a pretty yellow gumball in a mason jar of macaroni.

"I suppose that's reasonable. But don't think for a flaming minute that you'll ever go topside again. That was a very stupid little stunt you pulled, Laverne," LPOD said. "Fortunately, it really didn't impact much at the end of the day. Hell marches on. I need the song by next week, Laverne. He leaned down toward me—way too close for comfort—and said, "It better be good."

LPOD sneered and leered menacingly.

"So what's the show about?" I asked.

"I'm very proud to say that I've outdone myself this time, Laverne. The show is called Hell Firings and it focuses on something that's been happening a lot *without* our help. We're just going to throw some kerosene on the blaze!"

He roared with laughter. The other two demons laughed along again, the sycophantic weenies. Pazuzu socked Melchom in his scaly arm. I grinned, nodding respectfully.

After he gathered himself, LPOD continued. "For years now, an amazing number of businesses have been laying people off in droves just before the holidays. It seems that their lovely evil natures value business goals over human souls." He giggled. "Hey, maybe you can work that into the theme song, Laverne. We're going to go into business offices and help things along a bit! It's amazing how entertaining it is to see people fired! The executives sully their own souls, to be sure, and those who lose their jobs are that much more likely to be vulnerable to our pitches. And it's sooooo easy to make it happen if you soul whisper the right folks. Tell him, Melchom. You are so much better with the accounting details."

"Well, we were testing this with a company last year and got their delightfully scum-sucking executives to hand out pink slips to 20,000 people at Christmas time. All it took was pushing the fact that the timing would let them expense the severance packages. If they had waited until January, they would have started the new fiscal year with a huge expense sitting on their books!"

Pazuzu added, "Workihhhhng with greehhhhhhdy businehhhhhs peohhhple gihhhhhhhves uhhhhhs ahhhhhl sorts of wohhhhhhhnderful ways to spread ehhhhhhhvil!" He started snorting excitedly.

Unbelievable, I thought to myself. What an incredible way to ruin lives. Happy Frickin' Holidays. Lucifer's Layoffs.

"We've got Niccolò Machiavelli on board as a technical consultant," LPOD added. "He is going to add some entertaining little side banter to each show. That guy is really hilarious when you get him going. Now I'm open to other ideas, but I'm thinking the theme song could be a riff of 'Hit the Road Jack.' I can see a metal version of that playing as flames consume a fancy boardroom. Heh, heh, heh."

"Yeahhhhhh," said Pazuzu. Ever the yes-demon. He farted again, quietly, this time, but an incredible funk enveloped us almost immediately. Even the imps manning the Hot Wings machine started back in alarm.

"With that, I must be off," announced LPOD dramatically. "Pazuzu will talk with you further about the theme song, but Melchom and I have some work *redecorating* the Evilometer, you might say. We're going to make it more appropriate for the office!"

I could only imagine what that meant. Installing some sort of soul inbox, or maybe a stand-up desk that involved the executive being stretched on a vertical torture rack? Maybe a water cooler that contained some noxious, bubbling brew? Sulfuric acid?

Speaking of noxious, Pazuzu sidled in closer and began to launch into his vision for the theme song. Oh boy. Well, I was grateful that Melchom left with LPOD. That yellow gumball was safe for the moment. But as for how long, no one could tell. I sure didn't need to be working closely with Melchom. Things were just getting hotter and hotter.

That theme song, however, would never be written.

CHAPTER 39

MACARONI

After they took me back to my cell, I eventually dozed off into a fitful sort of sleep. I had a dream. Simone and I were flying through the air as eagles. Not the Glenn Frey and Don Henley, six number-one albums kind of Eagles. The ones with feathers. We were very high in the air when I flew toward her, then reached out with one of my feet and locked talons with her. It was sort of like, well, holding hands, but for some reason it felt like so much more than that. We then started spinning around in the air, gliding down, down, down, cartwheeling around and around. We were just above the ground when I woke up with a start.

As I lay there on the iron bed, the hot, scratchy metal digging into my back, I remembered seeing the same thing on a nature show once. Incidentally, in nature the eagles manage to unlock talons right before splattsville. It's a mating ritual truly fit for adventure seekers. Bungee jumping with babes. I guess it gets the blood moving.

Well, welcome back to *Hotel California*. I noticed with satisfaction that my guitar, amp and headphones were now in the corner of the cell across from my bunk. I was excited about getting them back, of course, but with a rush I remembered that I was now going to have to rub shoulders with Melchom on this thing. I groaned and saw him leering in my mind's eye.

That guy was probably the absolute worst demon for me to be around right now. Eligos would be bad, too, but Melchom was *the* worst. He hadn't been named paymaster of Hell because he was good at missing details. I had heard that even demons of the highest orders didn't want to be around him. They all had their evil secrets, of course, and Melchom could always peer deep into their dark, black-oiled souls and drag them out, wiggling and screaming at the light.

Just then my cell door crashed open. I leapt to my feet. Guess who. I think I unconsciously made a little groan. If they actually let you eat down there, I would have undoubtedly evacuated my bowels. Melchom stared at me across the threshold with his piercing green eyes. But he did not enter.

"I don't have the time, nor the inclination at the moment," he said. "But I am absolutely certain that there is something that you're trying to hide from me, Laverne. Given your recent history, I almost can't believe that you would be dumb enough to draw any, shall we say, *negative* attention to yourself, so I will trust it isn't anything of too much import?"

I was so horrified I couldn't speak.

"Ah, so I was right. In all my millennia in this place, I have never come across anyone thinking about a jar full of macaroni." He smiled sinisterly. "Well, we'll get to the bottom of that together, I assure you, Laverne. It is always best to unburden yourself, you know. Clear conscience and all that. We're big into that down here, as you know. So don't you worry. As soon as that theme song is done and LPOD doesn't care what happens with you anymore, we'll get there together. We have all the time in the underworld."

The door slammed shut. I collapsed onto the floor in horror, thinking "Oh, Simone, what have I done to you?" I wasn't concerned about myself any longer, but I couldn't believe I had gotten her involved.

BERITH

The Canaanites revered Berith
as their lord of covenant. Later,
they elevated him to the plumb
position of god of death. He has
a photographic memory, which
certainly comes in handy in his day
jobs as both Chief Secretary of Hell
and head of its archives. Twenty-
six legions of demons serve under
his command, and commanding he
is in his red uniform riding a red
horse and wearing a golden crown
on his head.

Berith is one of the 72 Spirits
of Solomon—number 63, to be
precise. King Solomon trapped the
72 rebellious demons within a brass
container, which he then threw
into a Babylonian lake so that no
one would be able to tap into the
powers it held. While searching for
the container, some ham-handed
Babylonians broke it and the
demons escaped.

Berith is the Hebrew word
for covenant. Baal Berith was
worshiped in Berith (Beirut),
Phoenicia. Alchemists knew
Berith as the element that would
transmute all metals into gold

Aliases

****

Balberith
Baalberith
Baal-Berith
Beal
Berithi
Bofry
Bolfry
Bolfri

Abilities

****

Berith can:
*
Lure men to commit blasphemy
*
*Use his photographic memory
to recount the past in excruciating
(and often ridiculously tedious)
detail*
*
*Answer questions about
the future*
*
*Turn all metals into fool's gold
(the alchemists were awfully
wrong on that one)*
*
*Lend clarity of sound and
ease of elocution to the voices
of singers*

****

MY PART

"Christmas as a concept has been a remarkably persistent, pernicious, powerful custom despite all of our best efforts over the past two millennia or so," said Berith, the pompous, fussy, red-garbed demon who had been assigned to help me brainstorm lyrics for the new theme song. As Chief Secretary of Hell, he was a font of good ideas, but he could wander terribly. It was incredibly frustrating. He also had a fondness for gratuitous alliteration, which made his rants even more annoying.

"Things always seem to happen. It's the oddest thing, Laverne. We have been consistently imaginative in creating insidious initiatives to injure, impair—and yes, might I say even incapacitate—the terrible tradition of Christmas," he said with an air of futility, his eyes rolling up and his head slowly shaking back and forth.

"It really goes back to the earliest days," he said, barely pausing for a breath. "We were initially very successful in splitting those crazy, cretinous Christians who created Christmas. The Romans and Western Europeans pushed for

December 25 as the date, and those from the eastern cities of Jerusalem, Alexandria, and Antioch pushed for January 6. Then, of course, those sneaky 25ers threw the easterners the Epiphany as a consolation prize. Oh sure, THAT's when the three kings came to commemorate the birth. Oh sure. How *convenient*. In reality those kings couldn't have ever travelled together. They totally hated each other's guts!"

He seemed to be getting really agitated, so I kept my mouth shut.

"We were also successful with things like the establishment of France's Feast of the Fools. I just love that name. In medieval times we helped foment that fantastic farce that really detracted from Christmas. Young clerics would mock sacred ceremonies, dress like women, and play dice on church altars. It was marvelous and merry—and very shifty and shady of us!

"Then, in Scotland we managed to manipulate officials into enacting laws that called for the arrest and prosecution of people baking seasonal treats, being hospitable to one's neighbors, and the playing of, dancing to, and singing of all nasty Christmas carols!

"Seriously?" I asked. "That can't be true!"

"It is, my disbelieving boob of a boy. And that's not all. We got the Puritans of North America to fine anyone celebrating Christmas the princely price of a full five shillings."

"Now that certainly cannot be true!" I protested. "The Puritans?"

He waggled his eyebrows at me and nodded.

"During the Enlightenment, intellectuals cynically sneered at the silly celebration and put the nix on nativity scenes. No more creepy cribs, they said. In Revolutionary France, under the atheistic Cult of Reason that held power at the time, Christmas religious services were banned and the three kings cake was forcibly renamed the 'equality cake' under official, anticlerical government policies. By 1800, it looked like we had the horrendous holiday on its heels," he boomed. He winked, sneered and licked his lips.

"Then in 1843, that half-witted hack Dickens published that inane, insipid, and irritatingly popular, *A Christmas Carol*." He paused for a moment tucking in his chin and making a face as if he was trying to gulp down his own bile. He gathered himself. "It was a turning point. I need not embellish or elaborate. Perhaps you don't know of its impact, but you must have read those seedy staves. Did you know it was organized in staves, rather than chapters—just as a piece of music might be? Ergo, a Christmas Carol?"

I'm sure I just continued to look dumbfounded.

He paused only briefly to smile condescendingly at me but didn't wait for an answer.

"We've had some victories since then, though. We were all thrilled, of course, to learn that the good ol' Soviet Union had banned Christmas in the USSR. Its most wonderful League of Militant Atheists encouraged school kids to campaign against Christmas traditions such as the Christmas tree. It even encouraged the little ones to spit on crucifixes to protest against the holiday. Hah!"

A sweet smile then took over his flabby face.

"And of course we were doubly thrilled when that hilariously heinous Hitler hijacked the holiday to further his aims. I never tired of remembering those cute, shiny swastikas and pagan symbols hanging from their trees. Now those guys could decorate! And those Nazified Christmas songs they created—they really got to me, I must say. They made your *'Jingle Hell'* sound like a cat food advertising jingle."

He looked up and to the side wistfully and then cleared his throat.

"That reminds me, we must make music! Ah, but it is getting late, I see. Let us continue tomorrow!" Knowing that I had less than a week to get the song done, I began to get even more worried. This guy was clearly not good at deadlines. I never did like group projects.

He hurled his red-garbed self onto his red horse and galloped off into the inky blackness. As the security demons shambled over to me from where they appeared to have been playing a spirited game of cards with a slimy deck that shimmered in the darkness, I sat thinking of the incredible challenges Christmas had overcome, and my personal role in some of them. In the end, how would the historical record of Christmas judge me? I shuddered and hung my head.

CHAPTER 41

SLIPPERS

The time I was happiest was when I had really decided to be a musician and we were getting our very first real gigs. County fairs, bars—lots of bars—and even a bar mitzvah. For that one we learned Dick Dale's Hava Nagila. Mazel Tov!

It was at that time that I developed a bit of a footwear fetish. For a little over year, all I wore was this one pair of bedroom slippers. I wore them everywhere—even in snow. They eventually disintegrated off my feet, but wow, I loved those slippers. They were that cozy kind of moccasin thing with the fluffy, wooly interior and an outdoor-worthy plastic sole. It was sort of my trademark.

As I lay in my bed half asleep and dreaming of those happy days, I could swear that I felt those moccasins on my feet again. It was a wonderful, comforting feeling that made me extremely happy.

I rolled onto my side, but something was terribly wrong. Where was the normal creak of the iron, cushion-less bed in my cell? This bed actually felt soft—way too soft. Could I have been swallowed again by one of those snack-food-loving dragons that live in the Hills of Wraith?

I cautiously opened my eyes. The first thing I noticed was the light. It was so incredibly bright that it made me wince. Slowly my eyes began to adjust. The second thing I noticed were the slippers. I was wearing a pair that looked just like my old ones, which I had last seen going into a garbage can in Ankeny. This pair looked pretty new but well broken in.

I sat up. I wiggled my toes. I looked around. I was in an all-white room. The bed was covered in a wonderful fluffy comforter, the pillows were puffy and soft, and the pillowcases and sheet looked like they were of a thread count that I had never even thought possible. I was also wearing some really, really nice PJs. A golden "Laverne" adorned the pocket.

The strangest thing was that the room's walls were covered with images of things that made me happy in life. There were pictures of family (the good days), pictures of musicians, some of my band's best shows (not sure how anyone got those), and even a picture of the great old gal who ran a little old family-run restaurant in Manitowoc, Wisconsin that made the best pies I ever ate in my life. She was holding two pies in her hands and smiling at me.

It must be a dream, I thought to myself. So I gave myself the old pinch test. Now here is the crazy thing. No matter how hard I pinched, I didn't feel pain. But I was aware that I was pinching myself, and there was sensation of pressure. At the same time, though, I felt nothing unpleasant. Odd.

I looked around. The room had one window covered with a—you guessed it—white drape. I pulled it back tenuously. Light streamed in. I peeked out. All I could see was blue sky and—where the ground should be—fluffy clouds. I was beginning to think ....

Something that sounded like a doorbell rang. I grabbed a super thick, white terry cloth robe from a hook at the foot of the bed, put it on, and walked out of the bedroom. The next room was a spacious living room filled with white and chrome furniture. Off to the left I could see a modern looking kitchen done in the same palette. The place looked like Mr. Clean's Cottage.

I went to what appeared to be the front door and opened it. On the front stoop was an unusually handsome blond guy wearing a bright white linen suit with a pale blue shirt open at the collar. My eyes panned down to what looked like white patent leather shoes with silver buckles. I looked at his face again. He smiled broadly. His hair was long and beautiful. To be honest, he looked like a total rock star. Then he told me his name, and I realized I was actually in the presence of one of the greatest rock stars of all time—figuratively speaking.

"Good morning, Laverne," he said warmly. "My name is Gabriel. You might have heard of me. Might I come in? I'll bet you have some questions. Oh, and I brought you a Starbucks. A grande cinnamon dolce latte. Your favorite, I believe?"

"Uh, yeah. Come right in," was all I could muster. I took the coffee and tried not drop it on my pretty white self.

I found out later that you never burn your tongue on hot coffee here. I also learned that Gabriel is the patron saint of those who work in broadcasting. And it is true that he plays a mean trumpet.

CHAPTER 42

GABE

Someone once told me this definition of Hell: On your last day on earth, the person you became will meet the person you could have become.

That isn't true at all. Hell is a lot worse than that. A LOT worse.

It took me a long, long time to adjust to the fact that I had made it out of there. In fact, I was in a daze the whole visit. I know I spent a good deal of time just staring at him and looking at that crazy suit. It almost glowed it was so white. The guy looked like he was in a Clorox ad.

I do remember him saying, "Call me Gabe!" which I found rather jarring. When you're used to hanging with the demons of Hell you don't hear a lot of folks telling you to use the shorter, more pally-wally versions of their names.

Of course, he also told me why I was there. It all centered on the power of redemption.

"You wouldn't believe the impact your little stunt in that Plush Productions store had on earthly affairs, Laverne. You're a bit of a star up here, actually. You and Simone managed to turn that whole Black Friday trend our way, and we are of course *eternally* grateful! Hah! Just a little Heavenly humor, Laverne. But seriously, you have no idea how viral that song went! It changed millions of lives – and after lives! And more importantly, we know from our spies that it got Satan to cancel that damnable show."

"Wow. Gosh, I had heard something about the cancellation, but I didn't realize ... I mean, that is unbelievably great! So that got me out of Hell and into Heaven? Are you ... sure?"

"It sure as Heaven did, Laverne!" He then went on, distractedly. "Hey, and Billy really owes you one! His career has taken off like a rocket since you gave him that opportunity! He's even got a Disney show called *Billy's Boulevard* and he's now impacting millions of little souls! Hah!"

"That's cool. I really wish him well," I said.

I didn't even feel a bit jealous about that. I guess that's what happens when you're in Hell and you suddenly find yourself in Heaven. The whole keeping-up-with-the-Joneses thing sort of loses its hold on you.

"Hey, have you seen your music room yet?" Gabe asked. He took me into a room off the kitchen. It was filled with the most amazing guitar collection. I found out later that it was a treasure trove of fantastically important instruments: a 1954 Fender Esquire, six collector-worthy 50s and 60s Stratocasters, a 1959 Gibson Les Paul, a '65 red Mosrite Ventures (the coolest of the surf guitars, in my opinion), a '66 Gibson Firebird, a '59 Gibson Flying V, a '55 Gretsch Duo Jet, and a variety of vintage Fender Jazzmasters, Jaguars, and Telecasters. Also, a slew of cool acoustics that I won't even begin to tell you about.

And the amps that were in there. My jaw dropped. It was really then that I was sure that I was in heaven. Oh, and sitting in a position of prominence was the black Strat from Hell and my little Champ amp. They both looked pretty beat up in that light, but I was so happy to see them.

Gabe caught me staring at it. "Yeah, we grabbed your gear when we extracted you. Figured you'd want that."

He smiled. I was absolutely floored, and—in fact—I really did sit right down on the floor.

Gabe chuckled. "I can see this is all a little overwhelming, Laverne," he said good naturedly. "I should let you hang out and relax a bit so you can get your bearings. Why don't I come back later?"

"Ah, OK, I guess. But can I ask you just one question?"

"Sure, Laverne. Go right ahead."

I looked up at him. "How did I get here?"

"Well, as you can imagine, it is a tad complicated and I'm not allowed to tell you too much. You undoubtedly have heard of our past battles with the fallen ones. I know that is part of the lore you learn about Heaven and Hell. And it is true. All I can say is that the battle continues, and—in essence—you were extracted by our special forces types. We call them the Alpha Omega Force. Obviously, this kind of thing doesn't happen all of the time, but for special cases ... well, you know." He smiled.

"Wow," I said, truly blown away. "I am so very grateful." I hung my head and felt like crying.

"Well, we'll talk more later, Laverne. But wait a minute. I have one more thing to share with you today. Simone is here as well."

CHAPTER 43

NEXT

You most definitely do dream in Heaven. You never have bad dreams. You sleep well, and you wake up rested. You always find something you want to watch on cable. The food is great. The drink is better. As I mentioned earlier, you never burn your tongue on coffee, and I never drink it black. In fact, I try very hard to stay away from anything black. It just tends to make me nervous. Oh, and let's just say there is absolutely no need for Cialis up here.

I pretty much wear those slippers all the time. I also wear my robe. A lot. My neighbors—we all live in a neighborhood that makes those Disney communities look like slums—have taken to calling me "King of the Robe." I have recut Roger Miller's old "King of the Road" song accordingly—you know how I like that kind of thing— and sometimes play it on an old Martin pre-war parlor guitar at neighborhood barbecues. At one of those parties, Jimi Hendrix showed up and played a rocking version of Ave Maria with his teeth, which were of course Pearly Gates white.

That brings me to the food. It's like being on a really high-end cruise ship, but without the lines. But I never eat the hot wings, even while visiting the amazing sports bars we have up here.

I've also jammed with some pretty big-time musicians up here. I probably shouldn't name drop but suffice it to say it's all a dream come true for a minor league rocker such as myself.

Simone and I were pretty inseparable for a long time. Then she just moved in and then she even agreed to marry me. Gabriel officiated at our wedding, and an 80s sitcom star named Leonard (ahem, think Love Island) was my best man. You make some pretty interesting friends up here. Simone's maid of honor lived on a Colorado ranch in the late 1800s. She knows some great old cowpoke songs that I'm trying to convert to rock versions.

The other day Simone and I were sitting on our white couch. I was modifying some cowboy songs on my white laptop and we were both drinking white Russians when there was a knock at the door. I went to open it and found a smiling Gabe on our doorstep, as sartorially elegant as ever in a white suit but with a pale yellow shirt this time. Very snazzy.

"Would you mind if I come in, Laverne?" Gabe asked as he cocked his head.

"Of course, Gabe. How are you?

"Fantastic as always! Simone, a good day to you as well!"

"Hi Gabe," she answered. "How wonderful to see you. Would you like a White Russian? Or would you like to stay for dinner? I'm making trofie. I know you love that!"

"No thank you, my dear. I'm actually here on business," he said as he sat down on an ottoman in our living room, his elbows resting on his knees and his hands clasped. His eyebrows knitted.

"You see, St. Peter has been cooking something up ever since you arrived, and I want to see if the two of you are interested in helping us with it. I'm going to visit our friend Leonard next."

Simone and I stared at him.

"St. Peter?" I said. "Wow, how did we get on his radar screen?"

"Well, as it happens, he took a deep interest in your story and has been kicking around some ideas with a number of us. As you might be aware, I am the patron saint of broadcasters, so I am a bit of an authority and have been involved quite a bit in these conversations. But I am getting ahead of myself."

We both looked puzzled. Gabriel paused, looked a bit uncomfortable, and then blurted out: "So we have this idea for a show ...."

COMING SOON

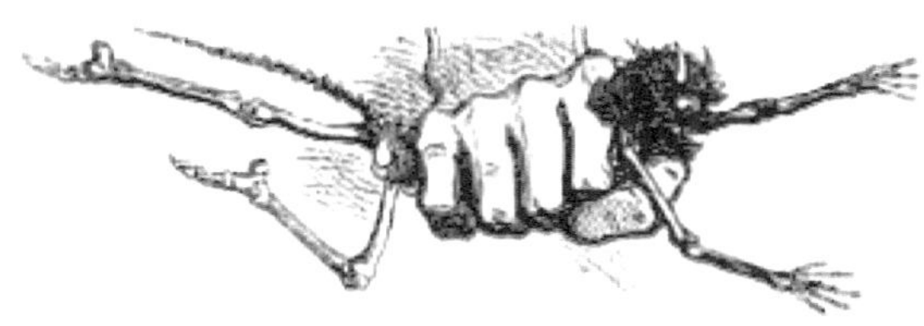

If you've enjoyed *Jingle Hell*, sign up at MagnusHuffam.com
to be informed when the next installment in
The Battle for Souls Series is available.

****

Magnus Huffam

Growing up in a bucolic Wisconsin county that has developed an ill-deserved reputation for murder, as a boy Magnus Huffam attended services at a small church. It was a healthy early exposure to the concept of good and evil, but he dreaded the stifling incense fumes spewed by the censers flung around during funerals and other solemn occasions. He currently lives in Chicago, where the influence of demons is more commonly felt. He believes that the good will always be victorious.

www.ingramcontent.com/pod-product-compliance
Lightning Source LLC
Chambersburg PA
CBHW021127070726
47591CB00014B/1680